As Jade started out the door, Reverend Weston reached for the bolt of fabric in her hand.

"I can manage," she protested.

"I'm sure you can." He took it, held the door, then followed her to her rig. After setting the fabric carefully in the back, he covered it with an old quilt to protect it from the dust of the trail.

"Thank you." She climbed aboard and caught up the reins. "But you might not want to be seen doing nice things for me, Reverend." She gave a meaningful glance at the window of the mercantile. "After all, what will the good people of Hanging Tree think about their minister being seen with a wicked woman? They might decide you're unfit to hold prayer meetings in their town."

"I wouldn't worry about my reputation if I were you, Miss Jewel. You'll have enough to worry about with your own." He gave her a dangerous smile and tipped his hat before sauntering away.

Dear Reader,

Our very talented and multiaward-winning author Ruth Langan can now add *USA Today* bestselling author to her many accolades, and we at Harlequin Historicals would like to congratulate her and fellow Harlequin Historical author Mary McBride for making it onto the list with their short stories in our OUTLAW BRIDES collection. Ruth's new series, THE JEWELS OF TEXAS, moves into full swing with this month's *Jade*, the story of a small-town preacher who surrenders his soul to the town madam. Don't miss this wonderful new story from one of our readers' all-time favorite authors.

In Kate Kingsley's new Western, *The Scout's Bride*, a determined young widow decides to accept the help of a rugged army scout who has made himself her unwanted protector. It's a marriage-of-convenience story you won't want to pass up if you enjoy a good Western.

This month's *Lady Thorn*, from Catherine Archer, about a Victorian heiress who falls in love with a sea captain, is—in the words of the reviewer from *Affaire de Coeur*—"impossible to put down." And Josh Colter and Alexandria Gibson discover they are both looking for the same man in Susan Amarillas's new Western, *Wyoming Renegade*. Susan's last two books have won her 5★ ratings from *Affaire de Coeur*, and fans have been eagerly awaiting this tale of two people who must choose between family, and love and honor.

Whatever your taste in reading, we hope you'll keep an eye out for all four titles wherever Harlequin Historicals are sold.

Sincerely,

Tracy Farrell

Please address questions and book requests to:
Harlequin Reader Service
U.S.: 3010 Walden Ave., P.O. Box 1325, Buffalo, NY 14269
Canadian: P.O. Box 609, Fort Erie, Ont. L2A 5X3

Ruth Langan

Jade

Harlequin Books

TORONTO • NEW YORK • LONDON
AMSTERDAM • PARIS • SYDNEY • HAMBURG
STOCKHOLM • ATHENS • TOKYO • MILAN
MADRID • WARSAW • BUDAPEST • AUCKLAND

ISBN 0-373-28952-9

JADE

Copyright © 1997 by Ruth Ryan Langan

This edition published by arrangement with Harlequin Books S.A.

® and TM are trademarks of the publisher. Trademarks indicated with
® are registered in the United States Patent and Trademark Office, the
Canadian Trade Marks Office and in other countries.

Printed in U.S.A.

Books by Ruth Langan

Harlequin Historicals

Mistress of the Seas #10
†*Texas Heart* #31
*Highland Barbarian #41
*Highland Heather #65
*Highland Fire #91
*Highland Heart #111
†*Texas Healer* #131
Christmas Miracle #147
†*Texas Hero* #180
Deception #196
*The Highlander #228
Angel #245
*Highland Heaven #269
‡*Diamond* #305
Dulcie's Gift #324
‡*Pearl* #329
‡*Jade* #352

Harlequin Books

Harlequin Historicals Christmas Stories 1990
"Christmas at Bitter Creek"

Outlaw Brides
"Maverick Hearts"

†Texas Series
*The Highland Series
‡The Jewels of Texas

RUTH LANGAN

traces her ancestry to Scotland and Ireland. It is no surprise, then, that she feels a kinship with the characters in her historical novels.

Married to her childhood sweetheart, she has raised five children and lives in Michigan, the state where she was born and raised.

To Kelly Shea Langan
and to her proud parents, Patty and Mike

And, of course, to Tom,
keeper of the flame

Chapter One

San Francisco
1867

"Come back to Texas with me, Ahn Lin." Onyx Jewel lay among the tangled sheets, looking pleasantly sated.

"You know I cannot." The young woman crossed to the bed wearing a flowing crimson kimono embroidered with Oriental symbols. She had sashed the robe carelessly, leaving as much revealed as covered.

He watched the fluid walk, enjoying the sway of her hips, the jut of her breasts, the subtle billowing of silk with each movement.

She was the most exotic creature he had ever known. Tiny, delicate and perfectly formed. Hair as black as a raven's wing, falling nearly to her hips. Pouting lips that begged to be kissed. And dark eyes that seemed to see clear to a man's soul.

"Can't?" His voice was little more than a whispered growl. "Or won't?"

Instead of a reply she held out a tray filled with an assortment of sliced fruits. Pomegranates, passion fruit, and mangoes were arranged in pleasing symmetry. It was possible, on the docks of this cosmopolitan city, to choose from the best the world had to offer. And here in the Golden Dragon, the city's most opulent pleasure palace, a man could find a world of delights. The rooms were filled with the finest Irish crystal, Oriental silks. The rugs beneath their feet were Turkish, the bed hangings Belgian lace.

"Eat," she said with a smile. "It will soothe the beast in you."

"It isn't food this animal needs." He caught her wrist, and she was, as always, jolted by the strength in this Texan who had stolen her heart.

Though she had built the most impressive hotel in San Francisco, a city known for its excesses, she had been careful to hold herself apart from all who came here to partake of its pleasures. Until Onyx Jewel. This larger-than-life cattle baron was the most fearless adventurer Ahn Lin had ever met. And though she had tried to resist him, in the end she had been completely won over by his charms.

"We have spoken of this before." Her voice carried the melody of her homeland. "Why must you continue to taunt me with what we can never have?"

He drew her fractionally closer, his eyes never leaving hers. "You said yourself it was a marriage in name only. For God's sake, Ahn Lin, you were only three years old. And he was your grandfather's best friend. By now he would be—'' he mentally calculated ''—seventy or eighty years old.''

''It does not matter. Until he dies I am bound to him, and he to me. I must respect the tradition—''

''Damn tradition! He'll never leave China. And you'll never return.''

She placed a hand on his naked chest and felt her heartbeat quicken. How could it be that she could want him again so soon? But she needed only to touch him and she was lost.

In a breathless tone she said, ''Do not ask of me what I cannot give. Is it not enough that you are the only man in my life? And that I have given you what I can never give him?''

At that moment there was a knock on the door. Just a light rap, but Ahn Lin withdrew and stood a little away from the bed before she called, ''Enter.''

An older woman in traditional Chinese garb stepped back to allow a graceful young woman to precede her.

''I bring greetings, honorable Father.'' The stunningly beautiful young woman bowed her head as her tutor had instructed, staring at a spot on the floor, and folded her hands as though in prayer.

Ahn Lin clapped her hands and the girl's head came up. But it was her father's voice, rich and warm with humor, that put the sparkle in her eyes.

''Come here, Jade, and give me a kiss,'' he called.

Ahn Lin stood to one side and watched the easy display of affection between father and daughter. And though the girl was small and dark haired like her mother, to the discerning eye she bore the unmistakable look of her American father.

This child would be the bridge between their two cultures. And though the mother would always be bound to that land across the sea, it was with a fierce sense of pride that she realized her daughter would know the freedom she herself would never know, the legacy of this bold Texan.

"How long can you stay, Father?" the girl whispered against his cheek.

"I leave in the morning." Out of the corner of his eye Onyx saw Ahn Lin stiffen. He knew that his words caused her pain. But there was nothing he could do about it. Ironic, he thought, that he controlled millions of dollars, and could command the ear of the president himself, but couldn't persuade one small, obstinate female to return with him to his home in Texas, so they could live like a proper family.

"Will I have a chance to visit with you before you leave, Father?"

He ruffled the girl's hair and brushed his lips over her temple. "You know you will. I have a special birthday present for you."

"A present?"

"It isn't every day Onyx Jewel's daughter turns sixteen."

She clapped her hands in delight and gave him one last kiss, then returned to her tutor's side. Assuming a formal pose, she bowed slightly and said, "I bid you good afternoon, honorable Father."

Ahn Lin bowed in return, while Onyx winked and blew her a kiss. She covered her mouth with her hand to stifle her giggles, and trailed from the room.

When the door closed, there was an uncomfortable silence. Onyx reached out a hand and pulled Ahn Lin to him. The plate of fruit dropped to the floor, but neither of them took notice. For they were filled with the knowledge that this one day of passion would have to last until next they could be together.

If the Fates were kind.

In a separate suite of rooms, Jade paced. She had seen her father arrive that morning, bearing an armload of mysterious parcels and boxes. As always, he had gone immediately to her mother's suite of rooms, where he had remained sequestered for the day.

Jade had been trained since birth to curb her impatience and hide her true feelings under a veil of inscrutability. But this day her emotions were incapable of being contained. She had been so distracted during her French lesson, her tutor had given up in despair. When Aunt Lily had sent her to the docks with Cook to purchase fresh fish, her feet had fairly flown along the streets. When she'd returned and found her father and mother still in their rooms, she had sulked and refused her lunch, even though it was her favorite—spiced chicken and rice.

Now, having been assured by her father that they would spend some time together, she was desperate for the hours to fly by.

Even her tutor's promise of a boat ride on the bay failed to elicit the excitement Jade usually felt. When they returned, Jade's cheeks were abloom, her eyes alight with anticipation.

In her room she found her parents waiting. Both Onyx and Ahn Lin wore identical looks of flushed pleasure.

Jade rushed into her father's arms. "I have missed you. You have been away too long."

"I know. Am I forgiven?"

She absorbed his quiet strength, his easy affection, and felt her heart soar with love.

"Why don't you open your gifts?" He turned her toward the bed, piled high with beribboned boxes.

With a laugh of delight she tore into the packages, to reveal elegant gowns, bonnets and parasols from New York, Paris and London. There were soaps in the shape of roses and violets. There were shoes made of calfskin, satin and fur. There was a hooded floor-length cape of raw silk, lined with ermine, for those days when the cold winds blew in from the bay.

With each gift, Jade's eyes grew bigger, her sighs softer. And after admiring each gift, she rushed to her father with another kiss.

"I thought you might wear this tonight," he said casually as he offered her yet another parcel.

She lifted the lid to reveal a traditional Chinese gown of bright green silk with a mandarin collar and frog fasteners.

"Oh, Father, I have no words. It is so beautiful."

"No more than you. You've grown into a beautiful young woman, Jade," Onyx said softly. "Almost as beautiful as your mother."

It was the highest compliment he could have paid her, and Jade felt her throat constrict.

"I'd like you and your mother to join me downstairs for a special birthday dinner," he said.

Downstairs. With the guests. It was a rare occasion indeed. "Thank you, honorable Father." Jade glanced shyly at her mother and saw that she, too, was surprised. Though Jade had grown up in this business, she was kept apart from it. "I would like that."

"Good. Your mother and I will go now. Join us when you're ready."

Onyx caught Ahn Lin's hand and the two strolled from the room.

When she was alone, Jade danced around and around, pausing only long enough to examine each of her gifts again. Then, when a maid arrived to help her dress, she felt the smooth slide of silk against her flesh. Her waist-length hair was brushed until it gleamed. The maid secured it with jeweled combs and draped it over Jade's shoulder, allowing it to spill across one breast.

When Jade examined herself in the looking glass, she caught her breath. She looked different somehow. Older, maybe. Or was it only her imagination?

Laughing, she danced from the room and down the stairs to join her parents. Finding the private dining room empty, she hurried into the more public rooms. There the air was scented with French perfume, incense and the rich sting of cigars. There was the deep rumble of male voices and the higher trill of feminine laughter. Glasses clinked. In the background music played softly. A lute, a violin, a piano. All carefully calculated to soothe away the cares of the outside world.

Jade stepped through the doorway into yet another room. Several men sat around a table holding cards. A woman in a shimmering, low-cut gown held the deck, dealing slowly.

As Jade watched the players, one man's head came up and his gaze locked on her. For the space of a heartbeat she couldn't move.

He was not dressed like the others, in the garb of a gentleman, but rather in the rough garments of the trail. There was an aura of danger about him. Except for a tattered cowhide jacket, he was all in black. Black shirt and vest over black trousers tucked into black boots. He wore a wide-brimmed black hat from which streamed a lion's mane of golden hair. His bearded face was in shadow. It was obvious that he had been on the move, and hadn't taken time to shave. A stubbly growth of dull red-blond hair covered his cheeks and chin, masking his features. But she saw his lips, full and sensuous, curve into a lazy smile. And saw his eyes gleam like a cat's. Smoke curled from a cigar in his hand. On his finger was a ring of twisted gold, with an amber stone that caught and reflected the light of hundreds of candles massed on the mantel. From the pile of chips in front of him, it was obvious that he was winning.

Jade had grown up in a house that catered to such men. None had ever affected her. But standing here, feeling his gaze on her, she couldn't move, couldn't even breathe. He was the most arresting, fascinating man she'd ever seen.

"Here you are. Cook has prepared a special dinner." Onyx, with Ahn Lin beside him, halted next to his daughter. "We're eating in that little alcove." He offered his arm, and Jade moved along at his side until they reached their table.

All through dinner she could feel the stranger's eyes watching her. Even when he seemed engrossed in the cards, she could feel his attention wandering to her. And though she didn't know why, she felt strangely exhilarated. Deliciously wicked.

When a servant brought tea and special little cakes with candles, Jade closed her eyes and made a wish, then blew out the candles.

"What did you wish for?" Ahn Lin asked gently.

Jade felt her cheeks grow hot.

"If she tells, she won't get her wish," her father admonished.

Grateful for his words, Jade expelled her breath in a long sigh. For in truth she had wished for something...someone...dangerous. Someone forbidden to her. Never before had she entertained such thoughts. And she knew she had no right to them. Not now. Perhaps not ever.

Onyx reached into his pocket. "I have one more gift for you, Jade." He removed a small jeweler's case. Lifting the lid, he said, "I want you to wear this always." He held up a gold rope on which rested two magnificent stones. One was black, the other green. "The black stone is onyx. The green is jade," he explained. "They represent the two of us."

Jade felt tears sting her eyes as her father placed it around her neck and fastened it. Sharing her emotion, he kissed both of her cheeks, then caught her hands in his and stared deeply into her eyes. "I can't always be the father I'd like to be. But know this, my darling. No matter what, I will always be with you. Even after I leave this world, I'll move heaven and earth to watch out for you."

"Oh, Father..." She was so touched, words failed her. She wrapped her arms around his neck and hugged him fiercely.

"I'm glad you like my present. I—" When Onyx felt a hand on his arm he straightened and looked up.

"It isn't fair." The man facing Onyx was impeccably dressed in a gray evening suit with high starched collar, gold and diamonds winking at his cuffs. In his hand he held a wad of money. But all the money in the world couldn't gloss over the fact that he was very drunk. "Here you are with two of the most beautiful women in the world...." The man's slurred words were loud enough to cause everyone in the room to turn toward him in stunned surprise. "And here I am all alone. You should be willing to share." He held out the money and pointed at Jade. "I'll take the younger one off your hands and—"

Onyx stood so quickly he sent his chair toppling backward. His hand fisted in the man's shirtfront, cutting off his words, cutting off his very breath. His face a mask of fury, his words choked with anger, Onyx growled, "You've just insulted my family. The young lady is my daughter. Now get out of here. And don't ever set foot in the Golden Dragon again."

The man brought up his hand, revealing something shiny that reflected the glint of candlelight. He jammed it tightly against Onyx's chest.

"Onyx," Ahn Lin cried. "He has a gun."

Reflexively Onyx shoved Jade and Ahn Lin behind him and drew his own weapon, though he knew it was too late. Before he could fire, the sound of a gunshot thundered through the room. For long moments there was an eerie silence. No one moved. No one spoke. Then, with a strangled cry, the man facing Onyx crumpled to the floor.

Across the room the man in black had upended the table, scattering cards and money everywhere. In his hand was a smoking gun.

For the space of several heartbeats Onyx and the gunman faced each other across the room, and the crowd seemed to hold its breath, waiting for what was to come. But instead of the expected gunfight, the man facing Onyx calmly returned his pistol to his holster, signaling an end to the incident.

Pandemonium broke out. While almost everyone in the room gathered around the fallen man, the one who had shot him watched without emotion. With the grace of a mountain cat he strolled to a side table, where he lifted a tumbler of whiskey to his lips and drained it in one long swallow.

Onyx dropped to his knees and checked for a pulse, then shook his head. "He's dead. Otherwise . . ." He left the words unspoken. But everyone knew that he would have been the one lying dead had it not been for the quick thinking of the mysterious gunman.

Jade, pale and shaken, heard only snatches of the excited words being spoken.

". . . been in here before. Name's Nub Harkness."

"Always causing trouble . . ."

"Can't hold his liquor . . ."

"You can be thankful Nevada was here tonight," someone said to Onyx, "or you'd be the one lying there dead."

With a thoughtful look Onyx crossed the room and spoke to the man whose quick action had saved his life. He offered his hand, and the gunman accepted.

A few minutes later the authorities arrived, and Onyx and Ahn Lin drew a little away to answer their questions.

Taking advantage of the confusion, the gunman made his way to where Jade, pale and shaken, continued to stand alone in the little alcove.

"I'm sorry your birthday party was spoiled." His voice, little more than a whisper, was low and deep, for her ears alone.

Jade's pulse was still pounding in her temples. In her befuddled state she couldn't put into words all that was whirling through her mind.

"Thank you." She felt tears spring to her eyes and blinked them away. "Thank you for saving my father."

He studied her, seeing the confusion, the numbness that signaled shock. Hoping to put her at ease he said lightly, "How old are you today?"

"Sixteen."

"Sixteen." His gaze slowly trailed over her and she saw a strange look come into his eyes. If any other man had looked at her like that, she would have felt sullied. But this man had a way about him. Some strange charm that held her in its thrall. Despite the fact that he had just killed a man, he seemed relaxed, almost casual.

"It's traditional to kiss a young lady on her sixteenth birthday. For luck."

Without warning he leaned close and touched his lips to hers. It was the merest brushing of mouth to mouth. But she felt the tremors ripple through her body, leaving her shaking. She was so overcome with feeling she couldn't move, couldn't even speak. All she could do was stand very still and absorb the shock of his lips on hers, and pray her legs wouldn't fail her.

When he took a step back, she strained to see his face, to memorize his handsome features. But all she could see were his eyes, hooded and mysterious, and his lips, curved into a dangerous, enigmatic smile.

"The drunk was right about one thing. You are the most beautiful woman in this room."

Woman. She was startled by the term. No one had ever before called her a woman.

Then he did something so unexpected she could do nothing but stand, as still as a statue, too stunned to even react. He traced his index finger around the outline of her lips, then dipped it inside the moistness of her mouth. As she blinked, he lifted his finger to his own mouth, as if tasting her. His eyes narrowed slightly.

Without another word he turned, then melted into the milling crowd.

Jade felt suddenly bereft. He was gone. The man who had saved her father's life. The most fascinating man she'd ever met had evaporated like the mist over the bay.

His bold kiss had stunned her. And his quick action had saved the life of the one who meant more to her than anyone in this world.

All she knew about him was his name. Nevada.

And the fact that he was capable of killing without emotion.

Chapter Two

*Hanging Tree, Texas
1870*

"**I** bring greetings, honorable Father."

Jade Jewel bowed before the rough pile of stones that marked her parents' graves. She often rode alone to the windswept site after the heat of the day had ended, finding solace in this primitive place that her father had so loved. How strange, she thought, that it was death that had finally joined them like a proper family.

When she had read of her father's murder by an unknown assassin, she had left the Golden Dragon in the hands of Aunt Lily and a well-trained staff and had hurried to Texas. What she had discovered when she arrived, cloaked in shock and grief, were three half sisters who, though vastly different, found themselves bound by a common thread.

She had grown to love those three strangers. Diamond, as rough as this land that nurtured her, always dressed like her wranglers, in buckskins and boots, a gun belt perpetually at her hips. Pearl, educated in Boston, was the perfect lady, in prim, buttoned-up gowns and a parasol to shield her delicate skin from the harsh Texas sun. And Ruby, an earthy beauty from New Orleans, shocked the sensibilities of everyone with her revealing gowns and casual indifference to propriety.

Despite their differences, Jade had found friendship, acceptance and, best of all, a feeling of family love with these young women. And so she had stayed on, adding her dead mother's ashes to this Texas soil, so that her parents were reunited in death as they never had been in life.

The evening sky was vivid slashes of red and gold against a backdrop of stark mountain peaks. A wild, desolate wind came keening across the hills, flaying the ends of Jade's hair across her cheeks.

All day the summer air had been hotter than a funeral pyre. Now, with night approaching, it was cold enough to sting the skin and chill the bones.

To the occasional passing wrangler of the Jewel ranch, Jade presented a fascinating picture. A tiny, delicate creature, she had dark almond eyes and hair the color of a raven, falling thick and straight to below her waist. In a land of gingham and buckskin, she preferred the garb of her mother's ancestors, a slim sheath of brilliant silk that fell to her ankles, with slits on either side for ease of walking. This day it was shimmering green, her favorite color, with a high mandarin collar and frog fasteners.

After a childhood spent in the luxury of San Francisco, this rough Texas landscape was alien to the young woman. But, she reminded herself, it was not nearly as difficult for her as it must have been for her mother, who had left the comfort of home and family in China to make a new life across the sea.

"What sustained you, Mother?" she whispered as she dropped to the earth on her knees. "Was it the ancient customs?" She moved her hand to the adjoining stones. "Or the love of one special man?"

She didn't need to ask what had sustained Onyx Jewel, the man who had stolen her mother's heart. Onyx was the most fearless man she had ever known. He had lived life to the fullest, until the day a coward's bullet had put an end to him.

From her carriage Jade retrieved an enameled plate, decorated with exotic symbols. Holding a match to a small stick, she dropped it on the plate and watched as smoke curled, followed by a sweet, thick fragrance. As the incense burned, she again knelt by the graves and closed her eyes, trying to calm her troubled spirit.

"I think it would please you if I would remain here in your home, Father. But how can I put down roots in Texas and still follow the ancient ways?" She remained on her knees for long, silent moments. "I seek your wisdom, Father."

In her mind's eye she visualized her childhood home in San Francisco, the luxurious apartment atop the city's most opulent pleasure palace. They had entertained kings and politicians, millionaires and actors. The rich and famous from all over the world had come there, to see and be seen. In that cosmopolitan setting, the daughter of Ahn Lin and Onyx Jewel had become skilled in the ways of the world. She had acquired a vast knowledge of languages and customs and intellectual pursuits. But she had no idea how to put such talents to use.

And then it came to her. The perfect solution to her dilemma.

As the vision faded, her lids fluttered, then opened. Her features relaxed into a smile of pleasure. "Of course. It is all so simple. It is exactly what the town of Hanging Tree needs. Thank you, my esteemed father, for sending me the vision. I shall begin work at once on the arts in which I have been trained. I shall reproduce here in Hanging Tree the pleasure palace of my youth."

Jade guided the team through the wide dirt road that was the main street of Hanging Tree. The elegant white-and-gilt carriage moved smartly past the blacksmith's shop, the stables, Durfee's Mercantile and Doc Prentice's infirmary. She sailed past the jail and marshal's office, past Potter's Boardinghouse, until the rig rolled to a stop at the very end of town, on a high, grassy knoll.

The air rang with the sound of saws biting into wood and nails being hammered. A collective shout went up as another wall was raised into place. Workers swarmed like bees securing the structure.

Jade stepped down from the carriage and stood watching as her future took shape before her eyes. Already she could envision the facade, with bright red winged arches, and a golden dragon standing guard on either side of huge, hand-carved double doors.

Once inside, a visitor would be transported to another world. Rugs, furniture, tapestries from the far-flung corners of the globe. Soft, muted music. Food unlike any ever tasted in Texas. And the air heavy with incense.

"There she is, Reverend." A woman's voice was raised in anger. "As brazen a hussy as you'll ever see."

Jade turned to see a crowd of townspeople trooping toward her, led by town gossip Lavinia Thurlong and her friend Gladys Witherspoon, with the preacher in their midst.

"Why would you bring such trash to our town?" Lavinia demanded, pointing toward the growing structure.

"Yes. Why?" The words, spoken by six or seven women, sounded like echoes.

"Why, we don't even have a proper church yet. And you're wasting money and precious lumber on this . . . this den of iniquity."

Half a dozen heads nodded in agreement.

"Mrs. Thurlong," the preacher said gently, "maybe you should give Miss Jewel a chance to speak."

"A chance to speak! We don't need to hear from the devil's own. I say we take a torch to this disgusting building before it can become a blight on our community."

Voices murmured in agreement.

The preacher stepped forward and faced the group of angry women. "Mrs. Thurlong, you agreed we would merely ask Miss Jewel about her intentions for the building."

"I don't need to ask," Lavinia said with an air of importance. "Everyone knows what she's planning. A whorehouse. Right here in Hanging Tree." She fixed Jade with a steely look. "And you can't deny it, can you?"

Jade swung away, turning her back on the crowd.

"You see?" Lavinia shouted. "She can't deny the truth."

Jade could hear the preacher's voice, low, persuasive. "All right, ladies. You've made your point. Now I think it's time to return to your homes."

"Oh, we'll go home," Lavinia cried. "And draw our shutters against the filth invading this town. But I warn you, Reverend, if you don't persuade her to take her disgusting business elsewhere, we'll have to resort to something stronger than words."

Jade clutched her arms about herself and listened to the sound of retreating footsteps and the murmur of voices as the crowd dispersed.

"They mean it, Miss Jewel."

At the sound of the deep voice, Jade turned. "Reverend Weston. I thought you'd left with the others."

She took a step back from the charismatic young minister, who seemed to have captivated the imaginations of all the females in Hanging Tree, both young and old. He was too intense, too... volatile. There was about him an aura of strength and mystery that bothered her. From the first time she'd met him, he had affected her this way. She didn't understand her reaction. But something about him made her uneasy. He was too tall, too muscular, too... potently male.

"I stayed so that we could have a little talk."

"I don't want to talk. I just want to watch my building take shape." She knew her voice sounded breathless, but she couldn't seem to control it. It wasn't the nearness of this man. It wasn't personal. It was simply that he had startled her.

He didn't look like a man of God. In fact, there were times—when he stood before the congregation, his fist in the air, his voice ringing with righteous indignation—that he looked like the very devil himself. With a mouth that was far too sensual for any man, and eyes more gold than green, he seemed exactly like a wild predator set free from his cage.

There was a restless energy about him that disturbed her.

He lowered his voice. "So far, the people are only resorting to words, Miss Jewel. I'm afraid when the building is completed you'll find yourself the object of a great deal more than words."

She was stunned. Her dark eyes flashed with challenge. "Just because I'm opening my business here in town?"

"It isn't just another business. To the simple people of Hanging Tree, it is the work of the devil." He studied her look of shock and knew that he'd caught her off guard. "They'll never permit it."

"Is that a threat, Reverend Weston?"

"A warning, Miss Jewel." He caught the full effect of those blazing eyes and felt a jolt. "You have no idea of the fervor of these people. I think you ought to be prepared for a fight."

"What would you have me do? Stop building now, before it's even completed?"

"You could turn it into something the people need."

"Such as?"

"How about a hotel?"

"The thought of calling the Golden Dragon a hotel is as ludicrous as calling my father a cowboy."

"It's said that before he became a cattle baron, Onyx Jewel was a simple cowboy."

She bristled. "Simple? Never. And the Golden Dragon will never be simply a hotel. In the land of my mother, her ancestors provided pleasure for emperors." Jade's voice lifted with pride. "The Golden Dragon will be a place where men from miles around can gather."

"Then be warned, Miss Jewel. The citizens of Hanging Tree will not take this lightly."

"I think it's not the people of this town you worry about, Reverend." She kept her smile in place, though her tone betrayed her growing anger. "I think you fear that the words you preach will not be strong enough to help them resist the . . . pleasures I offer."

His eyes narrowed. "I know more about these people than you do, Miss Jewel. They'll rise up and fight you on this. And the fighting could turn ugly."

"I should think that would make you happy." Deliberately ignoring him, she turned her back on him and watched the swarm of workmen. "You can become a hero in the eyes of your congregation as you lead them in the fight against the devil."

"I wouldn't want to see that happen, Miss Jewel."

"Neither would I, Reverend Weston."

Proud. Intractable. Those were the words that came to mind as he watched her. She would be a formidable opponent. But he knew from experience that she would be no match for the people of Hanging Tree.

"I hope you'll change your mind about the sort of work you intend to do."

"How can I? It's all I know. All I've been trained for."

He paused a moment, studying the proud tilt of her head. Could it be that in her innocence she saw nothing wrong with her plans? "I'll bid you good day, Miss Jewel." In loose, easy strides he walked away.

Jade continued to watch the workmen. But her heart was beating overtime. And the day had grown unseasonably warm. Anger, she told herself, not the preacher, always had that effect on her.

"Good afternoon, Miss Jade. I was just talking about your new business to the Reverend and Willy here." Rufus Durfee, owner of Durfee's Mercantile, nodded toward Wade Weston and a visiting rancher, who had brought him a wagonload of beehives in exchange for some sacks of flour and sugar.

Jade managed a smile.

Rufus hooked a thumb toward the end of town. "Miss Jade Jewel is building the Golden Dragon."

"You don't say?" The rancher squinted through the dirty window and watched the workers as they scrambled to secure the final wall.

Jade walked between two shelves displaying an assortment of canned goods and bolts of fabric. She heard the rancher ask, "What good's a place like that out here in the middle of nowhere? I mean, hell, Rufus, who can afford it?"

Rufus gave a muffled reply. "What do I care? As long as it ain't my money, I'm willing to allow Miss Jade to build anything she wants. Don't forget, the town's growing. Last year alone we had the visiting judge stop by almost once a month. And those banker fellows, looking to take over Chester Pierce's bank, after he got hung for shooting Onyx Jewel." He lowered his voice. "It would seem that Hanging Tree is enjoying a building boom. Besides Miss Jewel's place, Farley Duke has just finished work on his sawmill down by the creek. And there's a rumor that the railroad's coming to Hanging Tree. If it's true, there'll be cattlemen and railroad men and people from all over the country beating a path to our little town."

"The railroad." The rancher's voice grew loud with excitement. "Why, Hanging Tree could become as big as Fort Worth. Or Abilene."

"Exactly what I was thinking." Rufus warmed to the subject. "Maybe I should add to my place. At roundup time, cattle drovers could clean me out in a single day."

Jade smiled to herself as she selected a length of pale pink fabric for Pearl. She hoped the rumors were true about the railroad. If so, the Golden Dragon could become the most important watering hole in all of Texas.

Hearing footsteps, she whirled as Wade Weston walked up behind her. "Are you following me?"

"You flatter yourself, Miss Jewel." He reached over her head and removed a tin of tobacco. "In the course of any given day, you'll probably see half of Hanging Tree in Durfee's Mercantile."

She glanced at the object in his hand. "Tobacco, Reverend? I thought you were above such things."

At her attempt to bait him into a fight, he merely smiled. "I'm riding out to visit old Yancy Winslow, and I thought he'd appreciate a little gift."

"I should have known. You have no vices, do you?"

His smile grew. "None that I'd care to tell you about, Miss Jewel."

As he sauntered away, Jade glowered at his back before following at a distance.

"'Course," Rufus was saying to the rancher, lowering his voice for emphasis, "there always seems to be a dark side to a town's growth. I've heard a few stories lately that had me wondering what this town's coming to."

"How do you mean?" the rancher asked.

Rufus lifted an apron and began polishing his spectacles, enjoying the fact that his audience had swelled. Two women from the town had just entered. Lavinia Thurlong and Gladys Witherspoon glared at Jade as she approached.

"There's talk that a gang of outlaws might be in the territory. A rancher returned from tending his herd to find his wife and children dead, their house and barn torched. And that's not all."

"Go on, Rufus," Lavinia urged. Her chin quivered with excitement. She couldn't wait to pass along this juicy bit of gossip. "What else have you heard?"

Rufus took his time, enjoying the narrative. "Over in Crooked Creek a rancher was found shot in the back, his entire herd stolen. Some say it's the Garland Gang."

Though that meant nothing to Jade, she couldn't help noticing the reaction of Reverend Weston. He had gone very still.

"Can't be," the rancher said. "I heard that gang disbanded a couple of years ago, after one of 'em went to prison."

"I heard that, too," Rufus said. "But Marshal Regan thinks the killings sound like Ned Garland."

Rufus took Jade's money and handed her change, then turned his attention to the preacher. "You tell Yancy to give you a list of supplies, Reverend, and I'll have my boys deliver them next time they're out that way."

"Thanks, Rufus. I'm sure Yancy will appreciate it."

As Jade started out the door, Reverend Weston reached for the bolt of fabric in her hand.

"I can manage," she protested.

"I'm sure you can." He took it, held the door, then followed her to her rig. After setting the fabric carefully in the back, he covered it with an old quilt to protect it from the dust of the trail.

"Thank you." She climbed aboard and caught up the reins. "But you might not want to be seen doing nice things for me, Reverend." She gave a meaningful glance at the window of the mercantile, where

Lavinia and Gladys could be seen watching. "After all, what will the good people of Hanging Tree think about their minister being seen with a wicked woman? They might decide you're unfit to hold prayer meetings in their town."

"I wouldn't worry about my reputation if I were you, Miss Jewel. You'll have enough to worry about with your own." He gave her a dangerous smile and tipped his hat before sauntering away.

As she left the town of Hanging Tree, Jade struggled to put Wade Weston out of her mind. Why in the world should one small-town preacher cause her so much discomfort? He was, after all, smug, arrogant, overbearing. And far too perfect for her taste.

She would prefer an adventurer, like Onyx Jewel, the man who had won her mother's heart. Or—the thought came unbidden to her mind—a mysterious gunman dressed all in black, who would calmly shoot anyone who threatened her harm, then kiss her until she was breathless.

With an effort she forced herself to put aside such nonsense and concentrate on the work ahead of her. She would have to go to San Francisco soon, to see to the furnishings for the Golden Dragon. There was only so much she could do by mail order. The rest would have to be arranged through her connections in the bustling California city.

The sound of her carriage blotted out the steady thrum of horses until they were nearly upon her. Turning, she was startled to see a cluster of horsemen. Their faces were hidden behind bandannas.

And their guns were all aimed at her.

Chapter Three

The cold, hard lump of fear settled in Jade's throat, threatening to choke her. Recalling Rufus's tales of horror, she urged her team into a run. The pretty, gilded carriage raced across the dusty ground, jolting over ruts and rocks until, at times, it seemed airborne.

Even when she heard the sound of gunfire she refused to halt. Instead, she shouted to her horses, urging them even faster.

A quick glance over her shoulder showed the horsemen gaining. One rider, on a lathered mount, pulled ahead until he was even with her rig.

"Stop or you're dead!" he shouted, leveling his pistol at her.

When he saw that she had no intention of obeying, he whipped his dust-covered mount until it reached her team. Leaning far over in the saddle, he caught the lead horse's bridle and held on until the team came to a shuddering halt.

Horsemen surrounded her carriage, their guns drawn.

"Now, woman, step down," one of them called.

"Let's see what we worked so hard to catch," shouted another.

The men laughed until a glance at their leader made the laughter die on their lips.

He remained astride his mount. Instead of a gun he now held a whip in his hand. A bandanna covered the lower part of his face. Only his eyes were visible beneath the wide-brimmed hat. There was a simmering blood lust in those dark, feral eyes. Jade was reminded of a wolf about to devour helpless prey.

"Step down from that rig." His voice, rough and commanding, added to his aura of danger.

Fear had Jade's heart hammering, but she gave no outward sign. Instead, clutching her shawl firmly around her shoulders, she stepped from the carriage and faced her attackers.

"If it's money you want—"

"Oh, we'll help ourselves to your money. And...other things, as well." At the leader's suggestive words, his men began to laugh.

"Take off the shawl. I'd like to see what I'm getting." He began to uncoil his whip.

Jade stood her ground, clutching her shawl even more tightly about her.

"I guess I'll just have to teach you a lesson, woman. When I give an order, I expect it to be followed without delay." The whip snaked out, and in one quick, practiced movement snagged her shawl, tearing it from her.

His eyes narrowed when he saw what she'd been hiding beneath it. The jeweled handle of a small, deadly dagger glinted in her hand.

"You think you can use that knife against all these guns?" he sneered.

"Would you care to test my skill?" Fear clogged her throat, making her voice husky. But she had no intention of giving in to the terror that threatened. "Before your bullets can stop me, my blade will find your heart."

At her words he sat up straighter in the saddle, regarding her in silence. "I guess I'll just have to call your bluff."

He lifted his arm to crack his whip. At the same moment Jade tossed her knife. Reflexively he twisted in the saddle. Instead of finding his heart, the blade bit deeply into his shoulder.

"Why, you little . . ." He let out a snarl of rage as he pried the knife free and tossed it aside. Then he gripped his flesh to stem the flow of blood.

Before his men could react, a series of gunshots rang out, sending them diving for cover. Another round of gunshots sent the dirt spraying directly beneath the feet of their leader's horse.

"It must be a posse, Ned," someone shouted. "Run."

The leader gave one last glance at Jade, then wheeled his mount and beat a hasty retreat. With shouts and curses, the rest of his men followed, leaving Jade standing alone.

She turned in the direction of the gunshots, but could see nothing but a thick stand of trees. She waited, lifting a hand to shield the sun from her eyes, but no horsemen appeared.

"They've gone!" she shouted. "You drove them away!"

Her words were met with silence.

Puzzled, she bent and retrieved her knife from the dirt. It was still stained with the blood of her attacker. Clutching it in her hand, she strode toward the trees, calling, "You can come out now. We're alone."

The grove of trees was empty. There was no one there.

She turned to look in all directions, but could see no one.

She knelt and studied the dirt. It bore the unmistakable sign of a single set of hoofprints.

Could it be that there had been only one man? If so, he had been wise to keep his identity hidden from those gunmen. For they would surely have stood up to his gunfire and exacted revenge for his interference.

But why hadn't he remained to reveal himself to her? She had a right to know who had saved her life.

She wanted to thank him. And somehow reward him for his kindness.

After carefully studying the surrounding area, she returned to her carriage and took up the reins. As the horses set off at a brisk pace, reaction to what had almost happened began to set in. Despite the warmth of the sunlight, she couldn't stop shivering. Her body was racked with tremors. She had no doubt that, without the appearance of her unknown savior, her fate would have been the same as that of the other victims of this vicious gang.

But who had saved her? And why had he chosen to keep his identity secret?

"A mystery man. How romantic," Pearl said when Jade told her sisters what had happened.

Her husband, Cal, foreman of the Jewel ranch, tightened his grasp on his bride's shoulder when he heard the news, and drew their adopted sons, Daniel and Gilbert, closer. It was one more thing to be concerned about. One more reason for the wranglers to keep a close eye on the women and children. "We'll need to report this to the marshal."

Jade nodded. "If it weren't for my...mysterious rescuer, there would be something far worse to report."

"Mystery man. Hah." Diamond, ever the cynic, touched a hand to the gun at her hip. Her cowhide vest couldn't hide the slight swelling of her middle, the only indication that she was expecting a baby.

"What you need is a pair of six-shooters." She glanced lovingly at her husband, Adam, who returned her smile with a wink. "Then you won't need a man to save your hide. You can do it yourself."

"I have my knife," Jade said softly. "And I used it against their leader. But even a pair of pistols would not have been enough against those men. Without that mysterious gunman, I would never have survived."

"I wonder who it was," Diamond mused. "Most of the wranglers around here work for us, or for one of the other ranchers in the area."

"Perhaps a passing cowboy," Pearl suggested.

"But why wouldn't he reveal himself to me?" Jade demanded.

"Could be a man on the run," Adam said, recalling his own scrape with the law, when he'd been wrongly accused of murder.

Cal nodded. "A man outside the law wouldn't want anyone to know he was in these parts."

"You are all wrong. I know who it was, *chérie*," Ruby said to Jade.

Everyone turned to the young woman, whose lips were curved into a knowing smile.

"It was your guardian angel."

"What nonsense," Diamond snapped.

"Nonsense! You do not believe in spirits?" Ruby's eyes flashed. "In the bayou we know these spirits intimately."

"Well, here in Texas—" Diamond began, but a question from Pearl silenced her.

"Didn't you say you saw hoofprints?" Pearl asked gently.

Jade nodded.

Pearl turned to Ruby, determined that common sense would prevail. "I don't think guardian angels ride horses."

"What do you know?" The fiery beauty gave her sisters a haughty look. "Jade said the grove of trees was empty. Those prints could have been made hours earlier. You will need more than that to convince me that it was not a guardian angel that saved Jade."

As Jade made her way to her room, she mulled over all that she had seen and heard. She was more confused than ever. Whether it was a spirit, a guardian angel or a flesh-and-blood man, she owed her life to this invisible protector.

Wade Weston yawned and stretched before tossing aside his bedroll and getting to his feet. He had decided against returning to his regular room at Millie Potter's boardinghouse last night. Sometimes he needed to be alone. To get away from the fancy black suit and the starched white shirt and the polite words expected of a man of the cloth.

It wasn't that he didn't like people. Most of the time he enjoyed their company. Decent folks like Millie Potter and her three sweet daughters, April, May and June. And honest folks like Rufus Durfee and his fine, strapping boys, Damon and Amos. And lonely old folks like Yancy Winslow.

But there were times when he just wasn't fit company. When the black moods came over him, blotting out all the good, the fine, the decent things of this world. Then he had to pull away, draw into himself and keep his own counsel.

He tossed another log on the smoldering embers of the fire before placing a blackened pot on the coals. Soon the air was redolent with the deep, rich fragrance of coffee.

He lathered his face and ran the straight razor across his cheeks and chin in smooth, even strokes. Then he stripped and strode into the frigid waters of Poison Creek. After soaping himself, he began to swim. With strong, powerful strokes he swam the width of the creek and back. Pushing himself to the limit, he continued to swim back and forth until his muscles protested.

Breathing hard from the effort, he clambered up the slope and tossed back his wet hair, sending a spray of water dancing in the sunlight. With his skin still damp, he had to struggle into his pants. As he reached for his shirt, he caught a sudden movement out of the corner of his eye. He whirled.

Jade was there, seated in her carriage.

How long had she been here? From the strained expression on her face, long enough to have seen more than she'd bargained for, he thought. Her eyes were wide, her mouth slightly open in surprise. But to her credit she wasn't blushing. And in the blink of an eye she composed herself.

"You shouldn't sneak up without warning. If I'd been another kind of man I might have fired off a shot before I even knew who you were." Wade grabbed up his shirt and shrugged into it, tucking it into his waistband and buttoning it as he walked toward her.

Seeing the tight line of her mouth, he softened his tone. "Sorry, Miss Jewel. I didn't mean to be so abrupt. But you startled me."

"You startled me, as well." She couldn't seem to tear her gaze from his strong fingers working the buttons. When she finally did, she found herself mesmerized by the width of his shoulders, the muscles visible beneath the fabric of his shirt. She couldn't put aside what she'd just seen. He had the body of a rancher, or a cowboy. Hardly what was expected of a preacher. "I—wasn't prepared to see you . . . to see anyone here."

His stern features relaxed into a mocking grin. "Obviously I didn't expect to see you, either, or I would have been better prepared. Or at least better dressed." He nodded toward the campfire. "Will you join me for a cup of coffee?"

"No. Forgive me for intruding." She lifted the reins, prepared to flee.

He reached a hand to stop her. "Please, Miss Jewel. Don't run away. I'm afraid I reacted badly. I apologize. I really would enjoy your company."

As his hand covered hers she felt the jolt. And struggled not to show it.

Her reaction to this man puzzled her. He had already made it clear that he intended to oppose her. What had her honorable father always said about an enemy? *Better to face his angry words now than his gun later.* Perhaps she should try to befriend her opponent. Or at least soften his arguments with a few of her own.

"I suppose I have time for a cup of coffee." She stepped down from the carriage and crossed to a fallen log. "Do you often sleep in the woods?"

"Not often."

"I thought you rented a room at Millie Potter's."

"Usually." He poured two cups and handed one to her before taking a seat in the grass. "But sometimes I just need to be alone."

"Ah." She stared into her coffee. "I can understand that. I often find myself wishing for time alone."

"I suppose it must seem overwhelming sometimes, facing the prospect of a new business, while also having to adjust to three new sisters."

She nodded. "I haven't decided which is more difficult. The business, or the strangers who are my sisters."

Wade leaned his back against his saddle and studied her. One dainty foot was crossed over the other. Her gown of amber silk clung to her curves in a very beguiling way. She appeared tiny. Delicate. But he knew that her appearance was deceiving. There was nothing weak or fragile about Jade Jewel. Right now she was frowning, and he knew that he was the cause of that frown. Ordinarily he would have done whatever he could to ease her tension. But today there was a devil inside him. One that he was tired of fighting.

"What brings you to the banks of Poison Creek at this hour of the day, Miss Jewel? I don't think it's privacy you're seeking. Or a bath." Though the thought of seeing her bathing caused a pleasant heat low in his stomach.

"I was eager to see what the workmen had accomplished since my visit yesterday." The truth was, it had taken all Jade's courage to leave the safety of her ranch. But she couldn't permit a gang of villains to rob her of her freedom. And so, despite her fears, she had forced herself to venture forth. "I...thought I'd take a different route to town."

Wade heard the slight hesitation in her voice. "Is something wrong?"

"Of course not. Everything is fine. Why do you ask?"

He wrapped his hands around his cup and gave a negligent shrug of his shoulders. "I just wondered why you came in this direction, when it's so far out of your way." His gaze was arrested by the jewel-handled knife tucked into the sash at her waist. "And why you're wearing that for protection."

Seeing the direction of his gaze, she touched a hand to the hilt. "I carry this always, though I usually keep it hidden from view. It was my mother's. And her mother's before her. When my mother came here from China, she carried this to ward off evil spirits."

His lips curved. "Did it work?"

She gave a mysterious smile. "I don't know about evil spirits. But it saved her many times from men with evil intentions."

Wade grew thoughtful as he stared into his cup. "The world is full of men with evil intentions."

"I suppose you see a great deal of them in your work." She sipped her coffee.

"And what about your work, Miss Jewel?" He looked up, pinning her with those fiery eyes. "Don't you think you'll have to deal with evil men in the Golden Dragon?"

She felt the heat stain her cheeks. "That will be my problem. And I'll be the one to deal with it."

"It won't be just your problem. The presence of such men will become a problem for the entire town."

She gave a sigh. "I knew you would find a way to twist this conversation until it got back to my business and why I should forsake my plans."

"You'll find many in town who oppose you, Miss Jewel. What you're planning is offensive to them. It will attract the sort of people to Hanging Tree that often bring trouble. I hope you have good friends to stand by you."

Again she heard that thread of righteous anger. "It's what everyone hopes for. A friend to stand by us in our time of need." She paused, thinking about her experience at the hands of the gunmen. Without thinking of the consequences she blurted, "I discovered such a friend yesterday."

He watched her in silence over the rim of his cup.

"On my way home from Hanging Tree I was attacked by a group of armed men."

His eyes narrowed. "Did you recognize them?"

She shook her head. "They called their leader Ned. Their faces were covered by bandannas. But I know that they intended... harm." She saw the hardness that crept into his features. And the little muscle that began working in his jaw. Even a man of peace would know what armed, ruthless men did to helpless women. "All I had for defense was my knife. But I was prepared to use it." She lowered her voice. "Or die trying."

"You look very much alive to me, Miss Jewel."

She drained her cup, then set it aside. "The gunmen were driven away by the sound of gunshots. But when they rode off, I found myself alone. Whoever fired those shots didn't wish to be seen. But I keep asking myself, why? Why would someone go to the trouble of saving my life, and then leave before I could offer my thanks?"

"Perhaps you imagined the gunshots."

"Did my attackers imagine them, as well?" Agitated, she stood.

He got slowly to his feet, towering over her. Again she felt awed by the sense of tightly coiled strength in this man of peace.

"No, Reverend Weston. I know what I heard. Someone saved my life. And though I don't know him, I'm deeply indebted to him." She tipped her head back to look up into his eyes. Her own were troubled. "Ruby explained it by saying that in the bayou everyone believes in the presence of guardian angels. Is that part of your culture, as well? Do you believe it was a . . . guardian angel who saved me?"

He gave her a dangerous smile. "It might have been." The smile grew. "But more than likely it was a stranger just passing by who saw a need and responded to it."

"But why would he leave without revealing himself?"

His gaze fastened on her lips, and she felt the heat rise to her cheeks.

"I can see that this disturbs you, Miss Jewel. But I don't see why it matters so much. You're safe. You walked away unharmed."

The breeze caught a strand of her hair and flayed it against her cheek. Without thinking he reached up and caught it, watching through narrowed eyes as it sifted between his fingers.

Jade couldn't breathe. Her heart was thundering so loudly in her chest, she was certain he could hear.

When he realized what he'd done, he lowered his hand to his side, where he clenched it into a fist.

"And you've probably learned a valuable lesson about the perils of traveling alone in this desolate land."

She let out the breath she'd been unconsciously holding. Sweet heaven, she'd feared he would kiss her. And the truth was, she couldn't be certain whether or not she would have resisted.

"Now you sound like Diamond." Highly agitated, she stalked to her carriage. "Thank you for the coffee, Reverend Weston."

"Any time, Miss Jewel." He placed a hand beneath her elbow to assist her into the rig.

Her pulse speeded up and she blamed it on anger.

As she took up the reins he said, "I hope you'll be cautious on your ride into town."

"You needn't fear." She flicked the reins, and the horses lurched ahead. "I wouldn't want to test my guardian angel too often. By the time the Golden Dragon is completed, he may be the only one left on my side."

Deep in thought, Wade watched until her carriage disappeared below a ridge. Then he returned to the campfire and tossed his lukewarm coffee into the flames.

Chapter Four

"Reverend Weston, look what Agnes made for you." Lavinia Thurlong had a death grip on her daughter's arm, shoving her forward until she was standing directly in front of the handsome minister.

"It's a blackberry pie." Agnes blushed and giggled as their fingers brushed.

"Thank you, Agnes. That's very kind of you." Wade gave her a gentle smile and set the pie on the windowsill of Durfee's Mercantile. Once a week he held services in the back room. The people came from miles around to hear his ringing sermons.

Out of the corner of his eye he saw Jade step down from her carriage, flanked by her three sisters. He fought to cover his surprise.

"Agnes is the best pie baker in Hanging Tree." At the moment it wasn't her daughter's baking skills that interested Lavinia. The only thing she had on her mind was snagging an eligible bachelor for eighteen-year-old Agnes.

Agnes was a pretty little thing, with a headful of dark curls, big brown eyes and a dimple in each cheek. The trouble was, all the cowboys for miles around were sniffing after her. And none of them was what her mother considered proper husband material.

Now, Reverend Wade Weston, on the other hand, was handsome enough to make even Lavinia's heart flutter. And every mother knew that a man of God would make an excellent husband. After all, the town minister and his family always had a place to sleep and food on the table. Not like farmers, who had to scratch a living from the soil. Or cowboys, who were always off chasing a dream, or another herd of mustangs. And from Reverend Weston's sermons he was known to be kind, considerate, thoughtful. In short, every mother's dream.

"I guess she takes after you, Lavinia," Wade said, keeping his smile carefully in place as Jade trailed her sisters up the steps.

Lavinia blushed nearly as much as her daughter. With matching smiles the two women filed into the room and took their places alongside their neighbors.

"Morning, Wade." Diamond greeted him affectionately.

"Good morning, Diamond." He accepted her handshake. "Where's Adam?"

"Out with the herd on the north range."

"Send him my best." He turned to Pearl, who was lowering her parasol. "I see Cal didn't join you."

"He and the boys are with Adam. This time of year there's just too much to do out on the range."

"I understand." He smiled at Ruby, who was adjusting her shawl to hide her revealing neckline. "I'm happy to see you, Ruby."

"You would have seen a whole lot more of me if Diamond hadn't reminded me to cover up." She knotted the ends of the shawl and tossed them carelessly over her shoulder before sauntering inside the mercantile. "Wouldn't want to create a scandal," she muttered.

The eyes of every man in the room riveted on her as she followed her sisters up the aisle to a row of vacant seats.

Wade was still chuckling when he turned to Jade with his hand outstretched. "Good morning." He kept his tone deliberately bland, though he felt suddenly too warm.

This day she was wearing a gown of pale blue silk, with mandarin collar and black frog fasteners. Her long hair had been twisted into an elegant knot on top of her head, with little tendrils slipping loose to kiss her cheeks and the nape of her neck.

"I'm glad you came with your sisters. I was afraid you might begin to avoid Sunday services."

"And miss hearing you warn the good people of Hanging Tree about the evil woman in their midst?"

He nearly laughed at the sparks that shot from her eyes. She was daring him to rile the congregation. And he was a man who had always loved a challenge. But he wasn't here to cause trouble. He would rather prevent it whenever possible.

She shot a look at the steaming pie. "An admirer, Reverend?"

"It's Wade," he said with a wicked smile. "And the pie is from Agnes Thurlong."

Jade returned his smile with a sugary one of her own. "A fine choice. Agnes is shy and sweet. She'd never give anyone a moment of trouble."

Unspoken laughter warmed his voice. "I see you came to town prepared to goad me into a fight."

Jade lifted her chin a fraction. "I came today because Diamond suggested that Sunday assembly would afford me an opportunity to face Lavinia and the others who have begun a whispering campaign against me."

Wade wanted to tell her they weren't whispers. They had grown loud. And ugly.

"I'll warn you again, Miss Jewel. Tread carefully. Even neighbors can become a dangerous mob, given the right set of circumstances."

He saw the way her eyes narrowed, and realized his warning had fallen on deaf ears.

"I also came today to thank my guardian angel."

If he was surprised, he managed to hide it. "And how would you recognize this paragon?"

"At the end of your service you always ask if anyone has any news they wish to share with the congregation. I've been thinking that I would plead for my guardian angel to reveal himself so that I can properly thank him."

Wade couldn't hold back his laughter. "I'm sure such a request would bring dozens of men leaping to their feet for the chance to be...properly thanked by Miss Jade Jewel."

She felt her cheeks grow hot. "I believe you're having fun at my expense, Reverend Weston."

"I told you. It's Wade. And I'm not making fun of you. More than half the men in this town would give a great deal to have Miss Jade Jewel indebted to them."

"I think you have me confused with my sister Ruby."

"If you believe that, you underestimate yourself, Miss Jewel."

She didn't allow herself even a moment to bask in the glow of his praise. After all, he was merely being kind. It was his job to say such things to people, in order to keep them coming to his service. Besides, sooner or later he would show his true colors and take sides with the townspeople against her.

"I'll say good day. I'm sure you'll provide us with plenty of food for thought, Reverend Weston." She emphasized his title before pulling her hand free and brushing past him.

"I'll try my best, Miss Jewel."

Wade spent another half hour greeting the farmers and ranchers and their families who took advantage of Sunday-morning services to stock up on supplies and visit with their neighbors. While he made small talk, or listened to their litany of problems, he found himself glancing across the room to where a slim young figure in a silk gown the color of Texas bluebells sat beside her sisters.

A number of people nudged each other, whispering and pointing at the four fascinating Jewel sisters. But it was Jade who caused the greatest interest. Each day, as the Golden Dragon took shape, the rumors spread.

Whenever their eyes met, Wade felt a growing admiration for the woman who was the object of so much speculation. Whatever she was feeling, she kept her spine straight, her gaze level.

By the time he started his sermon, he had found his inspiration. And by the time his sermon ended, even Lavinia Thurlong and Gladys Witherspoon agreed that the preacher had never displayed more zeal.

The topic of his sermon had been the danger of idle gossip.

"Does anyone wish to share something with the congregation?" Wade asked at the end of the service.

When no one stood, he stared pointedly at Jade. Feeling the heat of his gaze, she refused to look at him. Instead, she kept her eyes lowered and studied her hands, folded primly in her lap.

She'd had plenty of time to mull over her intention. The more she thought about it, the more she realized that Wade was right. If she foolishly announced to the entire town that a mystery man had saved her from a gang, she would then have to describe in detail what had happened. And the thought of making public her encounter was most unappealing. It had been difficult enough just telling the marshal. Besides, throughout the entire sermon she had felt the hostile stares from the congregation. There was no way she wanted to draw any more attention to herself.

"Well, then." Wade gave them the benediction of his smile. "I hope you will all leave with a lighter burden than when you entered."

He walked to the door and opened it, then stepped out on the porch, shaking hands with the people as they took their leave. When the Jewel sisters stepped outside, he had a smile and a kind word for each of them.

Jade steeled herself as she was forced to offer her hand. "That was a lovely sermon." She absorbed the jolt as she looked into his eyes.

"I'm glad you liked it." His big hand engulfed hers. There was a hint of laughter in his voice. "I did it for your benefit. After all, you're going to need all the cooperation your neighbors have to give, once the Golden Dragon is completed." Before she could respond he added, "I thought you were going to ask about your mystery man. What happened, Miss Jewel? Lose your nerve?"

"I...thought about it and decided you were right. It would be foolish to make a spectacle of myself. I'm sure he had a good reason for not wanting to reveal himself."

"I think you did the right thing. Still," he added with a growing smile, "it would have been interesting to see how many men would admit to being your guardian angel."

She pulled her hand away and took a step back. Once again he was laughing at her. She found his sense of humor wearing thin. "Good day, Reverend Weston."

"Good day, Miss Jewel," he muttered as he turned to Rufus Durfee and his family.

With Sunday services concluded, most of the ranchers and their families enjoyed a brief respite from their rigorous chores. The children played tag around the trees, while the men loaded their wagons with supplies. The women spread quilts on the grass and gossiped with neighbors while laying out the food they'd brought from home.

"Come on." Diamond looped her arm through Pearl's, and motioned for Jade and Ruby to follow. "Let's get to Millie Potter's before all the food is gone."

Millie Potter's boardinghouse always enjoyed a rush of business on Sunday. Besides her regulars, like

Marshal Quent Regan and Dr. Cosmo Prentice and the other bachelors, there were those ranch families prosperous enough to indulge their taste for Millie's fine cooking.

Potter's Boardinghouse sat at the end of the dusty road the townspeople referred to as Main Street. The house reflected the woman who owned it. Neat as a pin, with the floors and windows sparkling, it boasted a formal parlor and a dining room big enough to hold a dozen or more comfortably. The dishes might have been mismatched, and a few of them cracked, but the food more than made up for it.

From the kitchen wafted the wonderful fragrance of freshly baked bread, and the spicy perfume of apples and cinnamon.

The door was opened by thirteen-year-old Birdie Bidwell, a neighbor of Millie's who helped out with the chores to supplement her family's meager income.

"Hello, Birdie," the sisters called as they stepped inside.

"Good morning, Miss Diamond, Miss Pearl, Miss Ruby, Miss Jade."

"Birdie," Jade said with a warm smile, "Pearl tells me you're her best pupil."

"Not for much longer," the girl said. "Pa thinks it's a waste of time for a girl my age." She held out her hands. "I'll take your shawls."

When Ruby reached for hers, Diamond shot her a withering look. At once the buxom beauty smiled and said, "I think it's a bit chilly. I'll just keep my shawl, if you don't mind, Birdie."

If the girl was puzzled, she kept her thoughts to herself. The summer sun was already high in the sky and threatening to turn the day into a sizzler. But if one of the Jewel ladies wanted to keep her shawl on, it certainly wasn't her place to ask questions.

As she hung the other shawls, her hands lingered on Jade's.

"What is this made of, Miss Jade?"

"Silk."

"It sure is soft," the girl said, running her callused palms over it. "It must cost a fortune."

"I suppose so." Jade gave the girl a gentle smile. "Maybe when you're older, you can buy a silk shawl."

As she walked away, Birdie shook her head. Silk was all right for a fine lady like Miss Jade. But the most she would ever hope for was a new gown of simple homespun. Birdie had never worn a new gown. All her clothes were made over from her mother's castoffs.

She gave one last glance at the fine Jewel ladies, then hurried off to finish her chores.

"Morning, Millie," Diamond called out as she entered the dining room. "Can you accommodate us today?"

"Good morning." Millie tucked up a stray strand of flaming hair before lifting the coffeepot. "Take a seat. You know there's always room for my best customers."

Her smile bloomed when she caught sight of the preacher.

"You're just in time," she called.

He made his way across the room, stopping to talk to the other guests before pausing beside Jade. He held her chair and settled in beside her. His thigh brushed hers, and she felt the heat all the way through her skirt.

"I would have thought you'd be at Agnes Thurlong's, having a leisurely Sunday meal with her family," Jade said.

"And sit idly by while they try to ensnare me?" His smile grew. "I thought I'd be safer here at Millie Potter's."

Just then Millie and her young helper began to serve the meal. As she paused beside Wade, Millie placed several biscuits on his plate. "I baked these especially for you," she murmured. "With extra sugar and cinnamon just the way you like them."

Jade nearly choked on her laughter. Everyone in Hanging Tree knew that Millie, a widow, was hoping to snag a daddy for her three little girls. And who better than the town preacher?

"Oh, yes," Jade said in an aside. "You're definitely safer here."

She savored her moment of victory while, beside her, Wade Weston dug into his meal in silence.

"That's an awfully big building you're putting up, Miss Jade." Marshal Regan forked eggs onto his plate and passed the platter to Doc Prentice. "Folks in town are concerned."

Jade felt the curious looks from the others. "Concerned, Marshal?"

"That your... business might attract the wrong sort."

Jade gave him a cool, reassuring smile. "I think you and the people of Hanging Tree will be pleasantly surprised with the results. The Golden Dragon will be a place of music, culture and fine food. I intend to run the Golden Dragon just the way my mother did in San Francisco."

"Sounds like a mighty big job for one little female," Doc Prentice muttered.

Jade lifted her chin and bit back the words that threatened. Instead, sipping her tea, she merely smiled. She would show them. She would show all of them what one little female could do.

Beside her, Wade Weston detected the tiny flicker of emotion. The lady was very good at hiding her feelings.

Doc turned to the marshal. "I hear there was another shooting."

The lawman nodded. "The other side of Poison Creek. Six outlaws ambushed Samuel Fisher on his way home from the sawmill where he'd been work-

ing for Farley Duke. Samuel was lucky to escape with
his life. If it hadn't been for his wife and four boys
riding up just then, he swears he wouldn't have made
it."

"Did he recognize any of the gang?" Doc asked.

"Not a one. Had their faces hidden behind bandannas. But from the sounds of it, they're the same
ones that have struck before."

"Maybe it's time to swear out a posse and go after them," Doc suggested.

"I don't like to take so many men away from their
families. Especially with a vicious gang like this."
Quent Regan washed down his meal with hot black
coffee, the fourth of the morning. "These outlaws
seem to enjoy killing."

"You think they'll strike again?" Diamond asked
quietly.

Quent shrugged. The badge pinned to his shirt
winked in the rays of sunlight streaming through the
dining-room window. "I don't know what to think.
But I'll tell you one thing. No one's going to terror-
ize the citizens of my territory. Not while I'm marshal. My deputy and I are taking every precaution to
protect the town."

Pearl shivered. "Such violence. I'm afraid I'll
never get used to it."

"It's part of Texas," Diamond muttered.

"It's part of life," the marshal added.

"But it doesn't have to be." Wade's words, though
spoken softly, held a hint of steel.

Jade turned to study him. In profile, he didn't resemble the man who had spoken so lovingly from the pulpit. With flaring nostrils and tightly clenched jaw, he looked as though he could lead a posse himself.

"It's easy for you to say," the marshal remarked, "when you carry a Bible instead of a gun. But you don't earn your living chasing outlaws."

"In a way, I do." Wade's tone softened, though the fire was still in his eyes. "You chase them to punish them, while I chase them to offer them the chance to seek forgiveness from those they've harmed."

"Well," Quent said, fiddling with his knife, "you may offer them forgiveness, Reverend. I offer justice. At the end of a rope."

Doc Prentice nodded, his pencil-thin mustache twitching as he smiled. "It's how our town got its name."

Everyone knew that the doctor, though a relative newcomer to Texas, had a fascination for the history of the town.

"Have there been many hangings?" Pearl asked.

"I've been told there were dozens," Doc replied.

"Was there an actual tree?" Jade asked.

"It's gone now." Doc Prentice helped himself to another biscuit and slathered it with Millie Potter's wild cherry preserves. "They say that old oak was here a hundred years or more. It stood on a hill just outside of town. The branches stuck out like long, spindly arms. Just perfect for hanging a man. The first hanging was for cattle rustling. Folks came from miles around. Afterward they stayed and had a picnic on the banks of Poison Creek."

He popped the biscuit into his mouth and chewed, then washed it down with a swallow of coffee. "After that it became a kind of tradition. Folks would flock to a hanging, then stay around to visit with the neighbors they hadn't seen since the last time."

Jade shuddered. "I can't imagine having a picnic after such a horrible event. It seems so uncivilized."

The marshal nodded in agreement. "Most of it was before my time. I hear it got so bad, folks were eager for the next hanging, just so they could have an excuse for another picnic. The sheriff finally had to request a federal judge be sent all the way from St. Louis."

"What good would that do?" Jade asked.

"He figured a cool head was needed to keep the townspeople from making hasty decisions that might cost an innocent man his life."

Beside her, Jade realized that the reverend had gone very still. When she glanced at him, he lowered his gaze. But in that brief moment when their eyes met she caught sight of a blazing anger. His hands were clenched so tightly in his lap, the knuckles were white from the effort.

Suddenly he pushed away from the table. "If you'll excuse me," he called to Millie Potter, "I have a lot of visits to make today. I promised Yancy I'd bring him some more tobacco. And I told the

Thompsons I'd stop by and share a Bible reading with their boy who was thrown from a mustang and suffered a broken arm. Since the widow Purdy took another spell, I thought I'd stop by there, as well."

"Sounds like you have a full day, Reverend." Millie filled the marshal's cup, then set down the coffeepot and wiped her hands on her apron before crossing the room. "But I should have expected as much. After all, it is Sunday. Will I see you later?"

He shrugged. "There's no telling. If I find myself too far from town, I'll just sleep along the trail."

"Then you'd better take this." She handed him a linen-wrapped bundle. "Just in case."

"Thanks, Millie." He turned to the others at the table and said his goodbyes.

Jade watched him pull on a cowhide duster and take his leave. She found herself wondering at his reaction to the marshal's words. She'd sensed anger in him. And pain. Not so surprising, she told herself. After all, he was, as Marshal Regan said, a man who carried a Bible instead of a gun. The thought of mob violence would be repugnant to such a man.

Still, for a man of peace, his reaction had been almost violent. And his violence, though carefully banked, was frightening to behold.

Chapter Five

It was late afternoon and Wade had been on the trail since breakfast at Millie Potter's, bringing whatever comfort he could to those who lay sick or dying.

As his horse topped a rise, he stared across the wide expanse of barren land to where a carriage stood tilted at a crazy angle. When he rode closer he found Jade standing alongside her rig, examining a broken wheel.

"Are you hurt?" He swung from the saddle and hurried to her side.

"No." She was so relieved to see someone, anyone, she could have hugged him. "Fortunately the team was moving slowly, otherwise I'd probably have been thrown to the ground. There's no telling how much damage might have been done." She rubbed a tender shoulder. "As it is, I was bounced around a good bit."

He studied her with grave concern. "Are you certain nothing's broken? Your arm? Your shoulder?"

He ran a hand across her shoulder, down her arm, probing gently.

She was surprised at the tenderness of his touch. And jolted by it. To cover her shock she muttered, "The only thing broken is that wheel."

Wade was genuinely concerned for her safety. And annoyed by the rush of feelings the simple touch of her evoked. With his fears relieved, he gave in to a wave of unexpected anger. "What in heaven's name are you doing all alone in the middle of nowhere? There isn't a living soul for miles. Did you want to tempt the fates? To see if you could outrun a gang of outlaws again?"

At his heated words, her relief was forgotten as her anger surfaced. "I don't owe you an explanation, Reverend Weston. But for your information, I was visiting the graves of my parents."

That stopped him, but only for a moment.

"Then you should have taken some of your wranglers along for protection."

"They have a ranch to run." She touched a hand to the knife at her waist. "Besides, I told you. I always carry protection with me."

He swallowed back a snort of anger. "As I recall, your knife was useless against the gang that stopped you on the trail."

She glared at him, but before she could protest he said crisply, "Maybe you enjoy tempting fate, to see if your...guardian angel will save you again."

"Instead," she said with a frown, "I have only you."

"Sorry to disappoint you." He turned his back on her and studied the broken wheel. "I'm afraid I don't have the tools to repair this. But I can take you to your ranch...."

She brightened.

"As long as you don't mind a few stops along the way," he finished.

She sighed. Her plans for the rest of the day would have to be postponed. But at least she wasn't stuck unhitching the team and riding bareback to the ranch. She managed a smile. "Thank you, Reverend. I'd be grateful for the ride."

He unhitched her team and led them to a shady knoll with grass and water, then tied them to a rope stretched between two trees. Assured that the horses were secured, he swung into the saddle, then reached down and pulled Jade up behind him.

The slit on both sides of her silk skirt allowed her to straddle the horse's back without tearing the fabric. It also exposed a great deal of her flesh, from ankle to knee.

Jade was surprised by the flare of feelings when her arms encircled his waist. As the horse broke into a run she was forced to hold on tightly. With her cheek pressed to his shoulder, she clung to him as the horse's hooves ate up the miles of Texas landscape.

While he guided his mount, Wade fought a battle of his own. He was achingly aware of the breasts flattened against his back, of the thighs pressed to his, of the small, delicate hands holding firmly to him. The wind caught Jade's hair, swirling it like silk around him. He inhaled the exotic scent of her perfume and found himself thinking things he had no right to. Things that quickened his heartbeat and made his blood run hot.

The direction of his thoughts threatened to distract him and make the rest of his day completely unsettled.

"It was good of you to come, Reverend." The widow Purdy lay in the big bed her husband had made for her more than fifty years earlier. "And what a lovely surprise to find Miss Jewel with you."

"You two know each other?" Wade had thought the widow, living in such isolation, would have no knowledge of this newcomer to the territory.

"Diamond had her wranglers slaughter a cow and deliver it to my place to see me through the winter. When she couldn't accompany them, Jade came in her place."

Wade arched a brow in surprise. It was another layer to the mystery that surrounded Jade Jewel.

"What brings the two of you together?" the widow asked.

"The reverend was just being neighborly. My wagon broke a wheel," Jade explained.

"That's just like Reverend Weston. He's been so kind to us. Please make yourselves comfortable."

Mrs. Purdy's skin was the texture of aged parchment after a lifetime of working the fields beside her man. Hair as white as the cotton fields in her childhood home of Louisiana drifted around a face that still bore traces of faded freckles.

Though her frayed cotton nightgown was modest, with high neck and long sleeves, she insisted upon draping a shawl around her shoulders out of deference to her houseguests.

"You'll have some coffee? My daughter, Martha, will fetch some."

"Yes, thank you." Wade hung his leather duster on a nail beside the door, then set a chair next to the bed for Jade, and another for himself. That done, he accepted a steaming cup of coffee.

The daughter, her own hair threaded with gray, took up a vigil on the other side of the bed, her knitting needles making a steady, rhythmic clacking that matched the shallow breathing of the old woman.

"Do you need anything, Mrs. Purdy?" Wade asked.

"It's kind of you to ask, but the folks from town look out for me. And Martha sees to my daily needs."

Mother and daughter shared a loving look.

"You're lucky to have family nearby," Jade remarked.

Mrs. Purdy nodded. "Martha's the last of 'em. Lost a son and son-in-law in the war, and both my parents. Thought I'd lost Beauford, too. But he came back to me. We came here back in '50. It was wild, untamed. Untried. But we were young and adventurous.'' She sighed deeply. ''All in all it's been a good life, Reverend. But I won't be sorry to leave it.''

''Hush, Ma,'' the woman beside the bed whispered. ''Don't talk like that.''

''Martha doesn't like to think she'll be alone.'' The widow patted her daughter's hand, then closed her eyes. ''But it can't be helped.''

''I've never been truly alone,'' Martha said softly. ''There was always Ma. And then Jed. And when Jed didn't come home from the war, there were the children. But now they've all scattered. And Ma...'' The knitting needles moved faster. She looked up with tear-filled eyes. ''Have you ever been alone, Miss Jewel?''

Jade shook her head. ''Not really. Though my father didn't live with us, he visited when he could. And there was always my mother. When I lost her, and my father, I discovered three wonderful sisters to fill the void.''

''You're very lucky.'' Martha glanced at the man beside Jade. ''Do you know much about being alone, Reverend?''

''Yes, ma'am. I'd say I know a lot about it.''

Jade turned to him. She hadn't given much thought to his life before his arrival in Hanging Tree. She had assumed there was a family somewhere. A father, mother, perhaps sisters and brothers.

''You've been alone a long time?'' Martha asked.

He nodded. "Most of my life, ma'am."

Was that a thread of pain? Jade wondered. She sipped her coffee and studied him more closely.

"How do you stand it?" Martha's words came out in a frightened whisper.

"I've never thought much about it," he said gently. "It's just the way my life has always been."

"That will change," the old woman said, her eyes suddenly opening to focus on him. "You're young, healthy. You'll find a good woman." Watery blue eyes fixed Jade with a piercing look before shifting back to the reverend. "And then you won't have to be alone anymore."

"I doubt that, ma'am." Seeing the looks exchanged between mother and daughter, he deftly changed the subject. "You say you came here in '50? I'll bet you have some stories to tell about the early days here in Hanging Tree."

"Oh, my, yes. We've lived through Indian raids, cholera, pestilence. We fought outlaws and survived some of the worst weather Texas had to offer."

"Did you ever witness any of Hanging Tree's famous...picnics?" Wade lifted the cup to his lips.

"Quite a few. I remember being surprised to see the festive atmosphere of the town's first hanging. At first the people held back, reluctant to witness a man's death by hanging, though most of us felt that anyone who killed or who rustled cattle deserved it. But after a while we started to see the picnics as an opportunity to come together with our neighbors.

You see..." She seemed determined to explain the town's actions, to justify their behavior. "Life here in the wilderness was hard. The only thing we knew was survival. There wasn't time for anything frivolous. But the way folks here saw it, the hangings were necessary to rid the community of killers. So we began using the hangings as an excuse to get together."

Wade paused before drinking. "Do you remember any particular hangings?"

Mrs. Purdy absently smoothed the blanket with her small, veined hand. "There's nothing wrong with my mind, Reverend. I remember all of them. There isn't much else to do on long winter nights but remember."

"Do you remember a rancher named Jessie Simpson?"

The old woman stared at the blanket, her hand smoothing, smoothing, before she shook her head. "Can't say as I recall." She peered at her guest. "Why do you ask, Reverend?"

"No reason. I asked Yancy Winslow about him. He said he couldn't recall the name, either. But he became quite agitated when we talked, and afterward he seemed concerned that his participation in the... town's picnics might keep him out of heaven when his time comes."

"Yancy was a bit of a hell-raiser in his youth, begging your pardon, Reverend." The old woman folded her hands, as if in prayer. "Maybe he en-

joyed the town's picnics a bit too much and is afraid
the Lord will close the Pearly Gates to him. But he's
getting on in years, and I wouldn't put too much
stock in his memory.''

In the silence that followed, Wade got to his feet.
Coffee sloshed over the rim of his cup. He quickly
drained it and set the cup on the table.

"I'll leave you to rest now, Mrs. Purdy. I'll stop by
next week to see how you're doing."

"Bless you, Reverend." She closed her eyes, weary
from the effort of making conversation.

Jade trailed behind as the preacher walked with
Martha to the door and spoke the words he hoped
would give her comfort.

Once outside he slipped into the duster, mounted
and pulled Jade up behind him. As her body was
pressed to his, she felt the sudden knife-edge of excitement. If Wade felt it as well, he gave no indication. He rode in complete silence. As though he had
turned inward. And was seeing in his mind all the
things his elderly hostess had just described.

And why not? Jade reminded herself. After all, a
preacher would be horrified by the thought of so
much violence and bloodshed.

She shivered as she contemplated the harshness of
this land that had claimed the life of her father. This
land that she had decided to call her home. This land
that was as much a mystery to her as the guardian
angel who had saved her from a band of outlaws.

Chapter Six

"I don't like the looks of that sky. Especially since we're still miles from your ranch."

At Wade's words, Jade shivered. To the north, black clouds roiled and twisted across the heavens, turning day into night. Even as she watched, the clouds rolled closer, blotting out the last of the light. Jagged flashes of lightning rent the darkness, followed by deafening rumbles of thunder.

Within minutes the sky opened in a torrent of rain. Jade pressed her face to Wade's shoulder, blinking against the downpour. He touched the hands clasped firmly around his waist. They were cold as ice. He had to find shelter. And soon.

With a sigh of resignation he wheeled his mount and headed in a different direction.

"Where are we going?" Jade's lips, pressed to his neck, caused a rush of heat that left him shaken.

"There's a deserted shack not far from here," he called above the rising wind. "We'll have to make a run for it."

Jade hung on tightly as he nudged his horse into a gallop. A short time later they came to a stop. Through the curtain of rain she could make out the shape of a cabin.

Wade swung from the saddle and reached up for her. She slid gratefully into his arms until her feet touched the ground. Then she ran ahead of him through the pouring rain, while he followed more slowly, leading the horse.

Finding the door ajar, she pushed it open and stepped inside. A moment later Wade entered. For long minutes he stood in the doorway, allowing his gaze to adjust to the darkness. His eyes narrowed thoughtfully as he stared around the room, taking in the sagging table and broken chairs, the empty hearth. Seeing Jade shivering, he strode outside and returned a short time later, his arms piled high with tree branches. He knelt before an old stone fireplace and coaxed a thin flame. As soon as the fire was started, he left her alone.

By the light of the flickering flame Jade studied her surroundings. It was an old cabin made of logs. A small hole had been cut in each wall, presumably to watch for approaching predators. The walls seemed sturdy and the roof offered protection from the elements. There was no floor, only hard-packed earth, giving it a musty odor. It was littered with shards of pottery and pieces of broken furniture. Wild animals had gnawed their way through faded mattresses stuffed with corn husks. But despite the debris, the little cabin was snug and dry. And for the moment it offered shelter from the storm raging beyond its walls.

Thoroughly drenched, Jade moved close to the fireplace and hugged her arms about herself.

"You're shivering." Wade's deep voice from the doorway had her whirling nervously to face him.

"I'll be fine now that there's a fire."

"You need to get out of those wet things."

She saw his gaze move slowly over her and she became acutely aware of how she must look. The wet silk gown was plastered to her like a second skin, revealing every line and curve of her body. Her damp hair fell like a black veil along her back.

Heat suffused her cheeks. Crossing her arms nervously in front of her, she eyed him as he approached, his saddlebags slung over his shoulder.

"I have a change of clothes in here." He dropped the leather pouches on the remnants of a scarred table and began rummaging around until he produced spare pants and shirt. These weren't the formal clothes of a preacher. Instead, they were the rough garb of the trail. He held out a faded plaid shirt. "I'm afraid this will have to do until your clothes dry."

"Dry?" She stared at his offering. "You expect us to stay here long enough for our clothes to dry?"

"From the looks of that storm, we'll probably be spending the night here."

"I shouldn't have to remind you, Reverend, what the people of Hanging Tree will make of this if they should hear. Especially if Lavinia Thurlong and Gladys Witherspoon get hold of such a scandal."

He actually smiled at her. "If you're worried about your good name, Miss Jewel, I can assure you I won't tell a soul."

"It wasn't my reputation I was worried about, Reverend. It was yours. If the women of the town hear that you spent your night with me, they'll run you out of town so quickly you won't have time to pick up your things at Millie Potter's place."

The devil was back, playing havoc with his common sense. He decided to see just how far he could push this smug little female. Instead of replying he merely stripped off his wet shirt and draped it over a broken chair. When his hands went to the fasteners at his waist, she spun away. But not before he caught the slight flush that crept up her cheeks.

He gave a satisfied smile. So, it would seem the lady wasn't as experienced with men as she pretended to be.

Jade heard the rustle of clothes, and the sound of his footsteps. And then his voice, warm with humor. "It's safe to turn around now, Miss Jewel. I'm decent."

She turned. Did he call this decent? She caught her breath when she saw that he was naked to the waist, wearing only tight-fitting black pants. Once more she found herself staring at the mat of fine, red-gold hair on his chest, the muscles of his arms and shoulders. She experienced the familiar dryness in her throat as her cheeks flamed. Why did this man have to have such an effect on her? She was certain her behavior would put her old tutor to shame.

She prayed her voice wouldn't tremble. "If you will turn around, I'll get free of this wet gown."

"You'd have me turn around, Miss Jewel? I thought you would prefer that I watch. Isn't that part of what will be offered at the Golden Dragon?" Seeing the way her mouth opened to protest, his smile grew. "Ah, well, if you insist."

Damn the laughter in his eyes. He had her so rattled she could hardly remove her soaked kid boots. Her fingers fumbled several times with the fasteners of her gown before she managed to peel the wet silk from her body. When she slipped her arms into the sleeves of Wade's rough shirt, she was grateful for the warmth. But it covered little, falling just to the tops of her thighs.

Crossing the room, she draped her gown over the back of the chair beside his clothes, then huddled near the fire, keeping her gaze averted.

Seeing her there, he took pity on her. She looked so small, so cold. So vulnerable.

"You can sit here." He spread the saddle blanket on the floor in front of the fireplace. "The fire will warm you."

"Thank you." She sank down in front of the blaze and felt the heat begin to still the trembling in her limbs.

Wade returned to the table, where he removed a linen-clad parcel from his saddlebags.

"Thanks to Millie Potter, we won't go hungry," he said as he unwrapped a hunk of salt pork, several biscuits drizzled with honey, and a precious bundle of coffee beans.

From his saddlebag he retrieved a blackened pot, which he set outside in the rain. In no time it was filled with rainwater. He added the beans and placed it over the fire. Cutting the meat into small pieces, he threaded them onto sticks and thrust them into the flame. Soon the little cabin was filled with the rich aroma of coffee and the tempting fragrance of sizzling meat.

Taking a place beside Jade, he set down the biscuits, withdrew the sticks from the fire and handed one to her. "Sorry it's such simple fare."

She tasted, then smiled. "It isn't simple at all. I don't believe I've ever tasted anything so wonderful."

They ate their fill of meat and biscuits, then shared a single cup of hot black coffee.

"Do you cook, Miss Jewel?" He leaned back on one elbow, drinking his fill before passing the cup to her. It was pleasant sitting here, snug and dry, sharing food and conversation with this fascinating woman. He studied her profile.

She sat cross-legged on the blanket, her back straight, her face turned to the fire. "Not very often. Carmelita and Cookie do all the cooking at the ranch. But sometimes, when I have a desire to taste the foods of my childhood, I sneak into the kitchen and make spiced chicken."

"Where do you get the spices?"

"I brought a small packet with me from San Francisco." She smiled suddenly and the whole cabin seemed brighter. "Did you know that you can buy anything in San Francisco?"

"Um-hmm." He didn't trust his voice. She had the most stunning face he'd ever seen. Small, perfect features. Exquisite almond eyes. Turned-up nose. Hair as black as a raven's wing, long enough, thick enough for a man to get lost in. And then there were her lips. Full, sculpted lips just made for kissing.

"Have you been to San Francisco?" she asked.

He made a great show of accepting the cup from her hands and drinking before he responded casually, "Once or twice. Tell me about your home."

Her smile was warmer now. This was a subject she would never tire of. "My father called the Golden Dragon a beautiful, exotic island in a sea of misery. As you can see," she said with a shy smile, "he didn't like San Francisco nearly as much as his beloved Texas."

"If he felt that way, why did he continue to return to it?"

She smiled knowingly at Wade's question. "It wasn't the city that brought Onyx Jewel back. It was my mother. He tried to convince her to leave, to return to Texas with him. But, though he held her heart, she refused. She called the Golden Dragon her finest creation, next to me."

Wade leaned back, enjoying the melodious voice with the formal inflection. She had a habit of lowering her lashes, as though carefully studying the floor, then unexpectedly focusing her gaze on him with an intensity that was blinding.

She broke into his thoughts. "How did you like San Francisco?"

"A beautiful city." Almost to himself he said, "A man could lose himself there and never be found." He pulled himself back from his dark thoughts. "You miss it very much, don't you?"

She nodded.

"Then why do you stay here? Why not return to the city you love?"

"It was my father's fondest wish that my mother and I would make our home here with him."

"But he's gone." Wade passed the cup back to her and struggled to ignore the tingling as their fingers touched. "Why not return to the place that owns your heart?"

"This is my home now. With my father's other daughters, I have found family. And even though my father is gone, I feel close to him here. I believe it pleases him to know I plan to stay."

"Sounds like Onyx Jewel is directing your life from his grave."

She merely smiled, touching a hand to the rope of gold around her neck. "Perhaps he is. Perhaps we are all ruled by the events of our childhood."

She saw his eyes narrow slightly.

She offered him the cup, and when he took it, she smiled up into his eyes. "What about your childhood? Where did you grow up?"

There was no answering smile in his eyes. She was puzzled by what she saw there. Pain. Anger. And then a gradual withdrawal until there was nothing.

"I guess I've seen just about all the West," he muttered as he drained the cup and set it aside.

"Is there no place you call home?"

"No place." His tone was hard, the words clipped. "I'm like the tumbleweed. Wherever I land, that's where I sink down roots until the next breeze catches me."

"So you have no plans to remain in Hanging Tree? What about the people who have come to depend upon you?"

"They're good people. I care about them." He shrugged. His tone hardened. "But who knows how long it will be before the wind charts a new course for me?"

She didn't know why she felt a wave of sudden annoyance. Perhaps it was his casual dismissal of the people who seemed so fond of him. Or perhaps it

was a reminder of the feeling of abandonment she
had experienced each time her own father left.

Standing, she began to prowl the tiny cabin, running a hand over the rickety table, pausing in a corner to touch a toe to the decaying mattresses. As she
turned away, a glint of light caught her eye. Embed-
ded in the ground was something shiny. She bent and
retrieved it, wiping it on her sleeve as she straightened.

"What is it?" Wade asked.

She held it up to the fire, where it caught and reflected the firelight. "A comb. A lady's silver comb.
Would you like to see it?"

He stood and took the comb, then stared at it for
long, silent moments.

"I wonder who lived here?" she mused aloud.
"And why they left?" She began to circle once more,
stopping to pick up several large pieces of crockery,
fitting them together to see the dainty flowers that
had been painstakingly painted on a large bowl. "It
would appear that there was a family. A father,
mother, children. They must have left suddenly." She
set the bowl on the table.

Wade watched as, one by one, the pieces fell away
until the bowl was once more just a series of shards.
"Are you telling me that you know all that by piec-
ing together an old bowl?"

She shook her head. "Look at the beds, or what's
left of them. A larger one for the parents, smaller
ones for the children." She ran her hand over the

rickety furniture. "The table and chairs were planed until there were no rough edges." She looked up, meeting his gaze. "That means the husband put a great deal of love and care into his work. And the dishes. Hand painted by someone who treasured them. But when the family left here, they left without their most prized possessions." She walked closer, until she was directly in front of him. Lifting a finger, she touched the object he still held in his hand. "A silver comb is far too expensive a treasure to be left behind. Unless the move was very sudden."

"You have quite an impressive talent, Miss Jewel. Do you often see the past?"

She shrugged. "Sometimes. When the spirits are unsettled. You can feel them here, all around us."

He surprised her by lifting the comb to her hair. Though her eyes widened, she didn't back away. Instead, she stood very still while he ran the comb slowly through her silken strands. It was the most purely sensual touch she'd ever experienced. Tremors rocked her and she had to struggle to remain motionless.

When she looked into his eyes, she thought she saw a spark, as if he, too, had felt it.

His voice when he finally spoke was low, rough. "Can you read the future as easily?"

"At times."

He put down the comb, and she saw his eyes narrow fractionally. "Can you tell if I'm going to kiss you?"

His words caught her by surprise.

"No." She started to back away.

Before she had time to think, his hands closed over her shoulders, holding her still. "And what if you're wrong?" he muttered.

Her eyes widened with surprise. Her mouth opened to protest. And then, as his mouth lowered to hers, the protest died on her lips.

The truth was, she wanted him to kiss her. Despite all her training, all the lectures she'd been given about holding herself aloof, she felt a quickening of her pulse at the thought of enjoying something forbidden.

She closed her eyes and offered her lips. But instead of the expected kiss, she felt his slight hesitation as his hands tightened on her upper arms.

Her eyes flew open. He was staring at her in a strange, guarded way. His gaze was centered on her lips, and she felt the heat as surely as if he were already kissing her. But still he hesitated, his hands moving in a slow, sensual rhythm up and down her arms.

Wade was shaken by the rush of feelings. He realized he'd made a terrible miscalculation. Just touching her was causing all sorts of trouble. If he kissed her, he'd be lost.

Calling on all his willpower, he released her and took a step back.

His hands were trembling. He thrust them into his pockets and turned, staring deeply into the flames. When he could trust his voice he turned back to her.

"I'd better see about some more firewood." He crossed the room and pulled on his rain-soaked duster. "It looks like the storm isn't ready to let up yet."

When he walked out into the darkness, Jade hugged her arms about herself. She could still feel the warmth of his hands where they'd touched her, stroked her.

Above the storm she could hear the sound of an ax biting into wood. How was it that he could arouse her so deeply, so shockingly, with nothing more than a touch? And then just as easily walk away and go about the business of chopping wood?

She picked up the silver comb and studied it in the light of the fire. The touch of his hand drawing the comb through her hair had been unlike anything else in her life. It had awakened feelings she hadn't even known she possessed.

She had tasted only one man's lips. And that kiss had been so long ago it was probably more imagined than remembered. But it had evoked the same longing, the same desire as Wade's touch.

With a sigh she returned the comb to the mantel and dropped to her knees in front of the fire. She stared into the flames as though they held the answers to all of life's questions.

What, she wondered, caused her greater turmoil? The storm outside? Or the one going on inside her heart?

Chapter Seven

Wade stacked an armload of firewood inside the cabin, then leaned all his weight into the door until it was closed tightly against the spray of wind and rain. It had been a relief to vent his frustrations on the pile of logs. Still, aching muscles were no substitute for what he really craved.

Then he turned and sat back on his heels, grateful for this opportunity to study Jade as she slept. One arm was curled beneath her, cradling her head. The other was outflung, as if reaching out to a lover. Such long, slender fingers. The thought of them touching him, stroking him, caused his throat to go dry.

It gave him an odd, pleasant feeling to see her in his rough plaid shirt, which revealed more than it covered. His gaze trailed along her bare feet, her trim ankles, then moved upward to long legs and shapely thighs. He studied the flare of hips, and the waist so small his hands could easily span it. In the glow of the fire he could see the shadowed cleft between her breasts. With each rise and fall of her chest, he felt his own tighten.

He wanted her. Desperately. And resented that fact. It was a struggle every time he looked at her.

He thought of all the sermons he'd preached about resisting temptation, and doing the right thing. At this moment they were just so many empty words. If he could have but one wish before he died...

Why was he tormenting himself?

He got to his feet and, tearing his gaze from the sleeping figure, stared around the little cabin. He envied Jade's peaceful rest, knowing there would be none for him this night.

Jade was instantly awake, though it took her several seconds to remember where she was.

The deserted cabin. The storm. Her heartbeat quickened. Wade Weston.

She sat up, shoving the hair from her eyes. The fire had been carefully tended, with a pile of fresh logs giving off their heat.

She stared around the cabin, and was surprised to find that she was alone. A glance at the window showed that it was still dark outside.

She got to her feet and peered out. The rain had stopped. The sky was streaked with the first ribbons of dawn light.

She slipped out of the plaid shirt and pulled on her silk gown, which had thoroughly dried. Sliding her feet into the kid boots, she strode across the room and out into the predawn chill.

At first she could see nothing but the darkened outline of a crumbling corral. But as her eyes adjusted to the dim light she could make out a figure moving around the perimeter.

Walking closer, she watched as Wade slowly circled the enclosure, running his hand along the top rail. Every once in a while he paused and stared off into the distance, as if seeing the mountains that were still cloaked in shadow. Then he continued his circuitous route.

As he drew close Jade caught sight of his face. Thoughtful. Pensive. His brows drawn together in a frown.

"Good morning," she called. "Did you sleep at all?"

His head came up. With an effort he managed to replace the troubled look with a bland one. "A little. And you, Miss Jewel?"

"I must have been more exhausted than I realized." She paused at the gate to the corral and waited while he slipped through the opening to join her. "I slept long enough for my gown to dry. Thank you for the loan of your shirt."

"You're welcome." He was careful not to touch her as he walked beside her toward the cabin.

At the nearness of him she shivered slightly and blamed it on the cold morning air. She glanced around at the dilapidated ranch, with its crumbled outbuildings and overgrown fields. "It makes me sad to think that this was once someone's home. And now it has fallen into such disrepair. My father told me that there were many ranchers who were forced to flee the rigors of Texas."

Wade's frown was back, deeper than ever. "Is that what you think? That they fled the hard work to return to a life of ease?"

She shrugged. "It's possible. What do you think?"

"I have more important things to wonder about, Miss Jewel," he said abruptly.

"Such as?" she prompted.

"Such as how soon we can take our leave." He crossed the rest of the distance to the cabin in quick strides.

"I suppose you're in a hurry to get back to the comfort of Millie Potter's boardinghouse."

"You might say that." As soon as he entered the cabin he pulled on the plaid shirt that Jade had worn for sleep. The scent of her lingered in its folds. His fingers slowed with each button as he inhaled the exotic fragrance. A rush of feelings swept over him. Feelings he hadn't even known he possessed.

Annoyed at the direction of his thoughts, he angrily stuffed the rest of his clothing into his saddlebags.

"I hope you don't mind if I use the last of your coffee," she called.

When he didn't object, Jade placed the blackened pot over the fire, then removed the remains of their food from the linen bundle. While she worked, she wondered about his anger. Was it something she had said or done? Or was he simply annoyed at this disruption of his schedule?

"It's a good thing we don't have to spend another night," she commented as she handed him a biscuit and several chunks of meat. "Or we would be out of food."

He could think of a more compelling reason not to spend another night. One that would have her blushing clear to her toes. But he kept his thoughts to himself as he finished the biscuit and washed it down with hot coffee.

A short time later he tossed his saddlebags over his shoulder and abruptly headed for the door. "We'd better get started, Miss Jewel."

She followed more slowly, giving a last glance around the tiny cabin before closing the door. Aloud she mused, "I'm almost sorry to leave."

"Why?" He turned to her with a look of surprise.

"There is something cozy about this little cabin. Something that speaks of love." Seeing the way he was studying her, she flushed. "My mother told me that I inherited this weakness from my father."

"Weakness?"

"These . . . fanciful thoughts that I occasionally entertain." Her cheeks bloomed with color. "My father once told me that it was not hardheaded determination that caused him to become a successful rancher in this wilderness. It was a need to leave all that was familiar and seek out an adventure that he believed would change his life forever. But once here he yearned for home and family, and spent the rest of his life seeking it. He called himself an incurable romantic. My mother, on the other hand, believed that it was unwise to have romantic thoughts in a demanding business such as ours."

"And you wish to be a clearheaded businesswoman like your mother?"

She nodded. "It has been expected of me since my birth."

"But aren't you also expected to marry? You said yourself that the business must be handed down from mother to daughter. If there were daughters, there must have been husbands," he said logically.

"Of course."

"And doesn't it follow that if there were marriages, there were romances?"

She shook her head. "Not at all. The marriages were arranged at birth."

Wade smiled at her joke. But when he looked at her more closely, he realized she was serious.

"Then your mother was married before she came to this country?"

Jade nodded. "To a man of her father's choosing. He sent her here, to set up a business and send the money back to China. She had always thought she would remain for only a few years. But once she opened the Golden Dragon, the months stretched into years, and she remained, though she vowed never to give her heart to any man. Of course,'' Jade added, ''that was before she met Onyx Jewel.''

Wade began to understand. ''So, even though she may have loved your father, she couldn't marry him, since she already had a husband.'' He had a sudden thought. ''What about you, Miss Jewel? Was your marriage arranged at your birth?''

She lowered her head and studied the toe of her kid boot. ''My mother desired it. There was a family in San Francisco who had come from her province in China. They had a young son who would be suitable. But my father would not permit it.''

For some strange reason Wade's heart felt free of a momentary burden.

As he started to pull himself into the saddle, he heard the thundering of hoofbeats and turned to see a dozen wranglers from the Jewel ranch, with Cal McCabe and Adam Winter in the lead. Riding between them was Deputy Marshal Arlo Spitz.

Cal's mouth was a tight line of worry until he spotted the exotic creature half-hidden by Wade's horse.

''Jade. You're here. Are you all right?'' he shouted as he drew in his mount.

Jade nodded. ''My wagon broke a wheel. Reverend Weston offered to bring me home. But a rainstorm changed our plans and caused us to seek shelter here in this cabin.''

Cal swung from the saddle, while the others remained astride their mounts, circling the couple. "When you didn't come home last night we were worried sick. We found your team and your carriage with the broken wheel. But the storm forced us to abandon the trail until morning."

Jade's eyes darkened with concern. "I'm sorry to have caused such trouble, Cal. You know that I would have sent word to you if it was possible."

"I know. I'm just glad you were able to find shelter." He patted her hand, then glanced up at Wade. "I'm beholden to you, Reverend. And relieved you were with her. I'm sure glad she spent the night here with you. At least I know she had nothing to fear."

Cal's words caused a rush of guilt. If the foreman of the Jewel ranch had any inkling of the thoughts Wade had entertained throughout the night he'd be holding a pistol in that outstretched hand.

Cal offered his hand in friendship. Wade had no choice but to accept.

Then the ranch foreman placed a hand beneath Jade's elbow and began steering her toward his horse, muttering, "I know you must be anxious to get back to the ranch."

It was all happening so quickly. One minute Jade had all the time in the world to thank Wade for his kindness. The next, she was being hustled away.

She thought of all the things she had intended to say before they parted company. But none of them sounded adequate. And so she managed to call over her shoulder, "Thank you, Reverend. I am grateful for... for all your help."

"You're welcome, Miss Jewel." Wade touched a hand to his hat, then clenched it into a fist at his side. As Jade and the wranglers left in a cloud of dust, he felt a wave of frustration. He ought to be glad that the source of his temptation had been removed. At least for the moment. But instead of gratitude, he felt a strange letdown. And a nagging sense that this thing between him and Jade Jewel was far from over.

Carmelita handed Jade a tray of roasted chicken spiced with red and green chilis. "I made these especially for you, Señorita Jade. I was so worried about you last night, thinking you were alone in that storm."

"Thank heaven you weren't alone," Pearl said fervently.

"It's a good thing it was Reverend Weston," Diamond remarked as she settled down to supper with her sisters.

Adam, Cal and the boys had returned to the north range, along with most of the wranglers, leaving the four sisters to share the night at the Jewel ranch. "Why is that?" Jade asked as she took a tiny portion and passed the platter to Diamond.

"If you were with any other man, the town gossips would have their tongues wagging faster than a herd of stampeding longhorns," Diamond muttered as she filled her plate. "As it is, I bet Arlo couldn't wait to get home and tell his wife. And everybody knows that whatever Arlo's wife knows, Lavinia Thurlong and Gladys Witherspoon will soon learn. And what those two hear passes directly from their lips to the entire town of Hanging Tree within an hour."

"But with Reverend Weston, your reputation is intact," Pearl added. "Not even the worst gossips could entertain the thought that anything... lurid could happen between you and such a fine, upstanding gentleman."

While the other two prattled on, Ruby studied Jade in silence, noting the slight flush on her cheeks, the way she kept her gaze fixed on her plate. "But the reverend is an attractive man, is he not, *chérie?*"

Jade's head came up sharply.

"Why, Ruby," Pearl sputtered in her most outraged tone. "That's simply scandalous. How could you say such a thing?"

"That he is attractive?" Ruby continued to study Jade across the table, and her smile widened. "He is not a monk, *chérie,* pledged to a cloistered life of celibacy. He is a man. And unless we are all blind, we must admit that he is a very handsome man. No doubt with a man's appetites."

"You're as bad as Lavinia and Gladys," Diamond said accusingly.

"It is not gossip I spread," Ruby said matter-of-factly. "It is truth, is it not?" Her dark eyes flashed a challenge to the others. Then she fixed Jade with a knowing look and lowered her voice conspiratorially. "So, *chérie*. Tell us. Did the handsome preacher offer to warm your cold hands in his?"

"Ruby, how bold of you," Pearl protested.

The bayou beauty turned to her with laughing eyes. "Are you suggesting that the noble Cal never tried to hold your hand, or kiss you, until he proposed marriage?"

Pearl's cheeks flamed bright red. She touched a napkin to her lips to hide her embarrassment. But she uttered not a word in her husband's defense.

"It is as I thought," Ruby said before returning her attention to Jade. "Men are men. Whether they earn their living by preaching or rounding up strays, they have a weakness for beautiful women. Now, tell us, Jade. How did you and the reverend spend the night?"

Seeing the high color that came to Jade's cheeks, Diamond pressed a hand over hers and said softly, "The first time Adam kissed me, I was so scared I wanted to run and hide."

"You?" Jade asked in surprise. This woman, born and bred in the wilds of Texas, was the strongest, toughest woman Jade had ever met. "You were afraid of a kiss?"

Diamond nodded. "Of course, the second time he kissed me, I kissed him back. But I was still pretty scared of the whole business. I remember thinking I'd rather have broken a wild mustang to saddle than have to deal with all those feelings I had tumbling around inside me over Adam Winter."

She looked into Jade's troubled eyes. "Is Ruby right? Did something happen between you and Wade Weston last night?"

For the space of a heartbeat Jade thought about confiding in these three women. They were, after all, the closest thing she had to a family. But her natural reticence, and her years of lessons in the art of gentle deception, would not permit it. Besides, nothing had happened. Nothing but a touch. A touch that had meant nothing at all to him.

She lifted a cup of tea to her lips and drank. Feeling her nerves begin to settle, she set the cup aside and faced her sisters.

"The reverend is a man of honor. If he were not, he would answer to my knife."

Satisfied, Diamond and Pearl began to eat. But as Jade ducked her head to follow suit, she caught sight of the sly smile on Ruby's lips. And knew in her heart that Ruby was no more convinced than she.

Chapter Eight

"Thank you for coming all this way just to see how I'm mending, Reverend. I enjoyed our talk, especially about the old days here in Hanging Tree, though I've forgotten more than I remember." The elderly rancher hobbled to the door of the cabin, leaning heavily on a gnarled stick, which his wife had fashioned into a cane. As Wade pulled himself into the saddle, the old man called, "And thank you kindly for the flour and sugar. Nellie will put it to good use. God bless you, Reverend."

Wade waved goodbye and turned his mount toward town. His saddlebags were considerably lighter after a day on the trail. He'd delivered tobacco to Yancy Winslow, one of Millie Potter's home-baked pies and a couple of live chickens to the widow Purdy, and flour, sugar and necessary supplies to Frank and Nellie Cooper. All in a day's work, he figured. And often more welcome and more needed than any sermon he could preach.

Of course, if he were to be brutally honest, there was another reason he favored the elderly with his visits. A reason far less noble. It wasn't their gold he was after; it was their memories. Memories of an earlier time here in Hanging Tree.

His horse crested a ridge, and Wade reined in to stare down at the lights of town. It was a peaceful scene. Smoke drifting from chimneys. The flickering lantern light from windows shimmering like fireflies. Even from this distance he could make out one or two familiar figures as they strolled toward the saloon or the marshal's office, moving like shadows across a screen. And yet, for all the familiarity, he felt disconnected from it.

The restlessness was upon him again. Or maybe it never left him. Maybe he'd been fooling himself. Maybe all he would ever manage was a few brief moments of peace before all the old demons would return to torment him.

This wasn't his town. Hadn't he said as much to Jade? These weren't his people. He didn't need to stay.

He closed his eyes and ran a hand over his face in a gesture of utter weariness. He couldn't return to Millie Potter's boardinghouse tonight. Nor did he want to spend a cold night under the stars along the banks of the creek.

He turned his mount away from town. And with the feeling of dread pressing down upon him like the weight of the world, headed away from civilization.

* * *

"That's the last of 'em, Miss Jade." Farley Duke, whose sawmill supplied all the lumber for the folks of Hanging Tree and the ranchers beyond, was also the man Jade had hired to be in charge of the workmen. He joined the others, who had stood back to survey their handiwork. Laboring from sunup until sundown, they'd managed to set in the last windows and hang the big double doors. "We can get started on the interior tomorrow."

"Thank you, Mr. Duke." Jade couldn't stop staring at the building. It was by far the biggest structure in town, standing as it did on a slight incline, and rising to two stories. For now, it appeared to be just square and solid and, except for its size, ordinary. But soon, she knew, an artist would add his magic, covering the green lumber with a coat of fresh paint. Dragons gilded with gold leaf would stand guard on either side of glossy, red-winged doors. And the interior would be like no other in Texas.

She sighed. It was time to make plans for that buying trip to San Francisco. But not yet. She wasn't quite ready to face the long journey. Hopefully she could put it off for a few more weeks.

As the workmen left, eager to return to home and hearth, she settled herself in her carriage and flicked the reins. She hadn't meant to remain in town so late. She still had a long ride back to the ranch. And dusk was already beginning to fall.

As the team carried her rig up hills and across meadows, Jade found her thoughts drifting once again to Wade Weston. What a strange, complicated man. On the one hand he seemed ideally suited to his profession. Without the encumbrances of home and family, he was free to give all his time and attention to those in need. He truly was charismatic. From his voice, low and deep, to those strange eyes, which could penetrate clear to one's soul, he was a commanding presence. And he was exceptionally kind. His generosity did not go unnoticed. Everyone for miles around sang the praises of the good Reverend Weston. Still, for all that, he was a man of mystery. He never spoke about himself. He had managed to evade her questions about his childhood, being careful not to reveal even the simplest details about his past.

Was it that air of mystery that attracted her? She thought of another who had piqued her interest. Even now, the thought of the stranger stirred her blood.

Jade was jolted out of her reverie by the sound of a gunshot reverberating across the hills.

Her heart leapt to her throat as she reined in the team in a stand of trees and peered through the gathering shadows. From up ahead came the sound of a man's voice uttering a vicious oath. This was followed by the rumble of several men's voices, and a burst of raucous laughter.

The band of outlaws! And she had nearly stumbled right into their midst.

Had they seen her approaching? Was the gunshot meant for her? Or for some other hapless traveler? She prayed it was only a rabbit or deer that had taken a bullet.

She strained to hear what they were saying. But the pounding of her pulse roared like thunder in her ears. All she knew was that the men up ahead had grown strangely silent.

Then a man's voice called, "What was that?"

"What?" another shouted. "I don't hear anything."

"It sounded like someone on the trail. Let's double back."

Jade was gripped by a wave of sheer terror. She must not let them see her. But it would be impossible to hide the creaking of harness and carriage wheels. There was no way she could sneak her rig past them. And if she turned around and tried to make it back to town, they would surely overtake her.

Fear made her movements stiff and awkward as she leapt from the carriage and fumbled to unhitch the team. Holding firmly to the neck of one horse, she slapped the second on the rump, sending it racing toward home. Then, pulling herself onto the other horse's bare back, she dug her hands into its mane and held on.

Unlike Diamond, Jade was far from being an expert horsewoman. But fear and determination made up for her lack of skill. Turning her mount in the opposite direction from the voices, she took off at a gallop.

"Over here," someone called, and several horses thundered after the riderless animal.

"No. This way," came another voice. "There must be two of 'em."

With a sinking heart Jade realized that at least some of the horsemen had caught sight of her and were on her trail.

Bending low over her mount's back, she deliberately veered into a heavily wooded area. Brambles and low-hanging branches tore at her hair and raked her flesh. The sleeve of her gown was ripped away, leaving a deep, bloody gash along her arm, but she took no notice of the sticky warmth as she urged her horse even faster.

The riders behind her were slowed by the dense undergrowth. Once or twice she heard men's voices, swearing, muttering. Each time, she managed to slip deeper into the woods. Soon the sounds faded into the distance, but still Jade continued whipping her animal into even greater speeds.

Brambles caught at her legs and shredded her skirt until it was little more than tatters. The bodice of her gown was torn and gaping, the elegant black frog fasteners torn away and trampled underfoot. Blood spilled from a dozen different cuts and scratches.

At last horse and rider burst free of the woods and found themselves on a wild, lonely stretch of land cloaked in darkness.

With every mile, Jade continued to glance nervously over her shoulder, terrified that the outlaws would somehow find her. She had no plan in mind now except to keep going, all night if necessary, to make good her escape.

In no time she realized, to her dismay, that she was hopelessly lost.

It occurred to Jade that all she really knew about this wild, primitive territory of Texas was the little town of Hanging Tree and her father's ranch. To a young woman born and bred in the city of San Francisco, this land was a frightening place. Especially now that night had spread its blanket of darkness, hiding the few landmarks she might have recognized.

Terror rose up like bile in her throat, threatening to strangle her. She swallowed it back and, shivering from cold and fear, resolutely urged her horse on.

As she came up over a ridge, the outline of a cabin loomed out of the darkness. When she realized that it was the deserted shack she had shared with Wade, relief flooded through her. She felt like weeping. At last, shelter. But at the same moment she felt a flicker of new fear. What if the outlaws should find her? Alone in this place, she would be at their mercy. And this time without the aid of her guardian angel.

As she slid to the ground she was startled by the whinny of a horse from the corral. Her hand flew to her mouth. What had she done? Someone was here. She glanced up to see a thin line of smoke coming from the chimney. Oh, dear heaven. It could be the remainder of the gang. If so, she had just walked into a trap.

"Turn around," commanded a deep voice. "And lift your hands where I can see them."

At the familiar tone she whirled. Standing in the shadows was Wade.

"Oh, Reverend Weston, thank heaven..." Her words trailed off as she was able to make him out more clearly.

He didn't look at all like a preacher. Instead of his usual dark suit and starched white shirt, he was dressed in the faded clothes of a wrangler or trail bum.

And in his hands was a very deadly-looking rifle.

It took Jade several moments to regain her composure.

"What...?" She lowered her hands and took a step toward him. But at the fiery look in his eyes, she halted. There was no warmth of welcome in those amber depths. And no smile on his lips. Instead he seemed as tense and wary as a predator.

He continued to stand in the doorway of the cabin, rifle in hand. "What are you doing here?" he demanded.

"I was returning home when I—" her voice trembled slightly "—nearly ran into that gang of outlaws again."

At once he lowered the rifle and took a step closer. "You saw them?"

"No. But I heard them. And I knew that they had heard me approaching."

When she told him what she'd done, there was a note of approval in his tone when he said, "That was quick thinking, Miss Jewel."

"I'm not sure I was thinking at all." She gave a wry smile. "I was desperate, and acted on instinct. But once I outran them, I realized I was lost. It was sheer luck that brought me here."

Now that she had found safety, she should feel relieved. Instead, a strange trembling seemed to have invaded her limbs. She started to take a step closer and stumbled. Before she could fall, Wade set aside his rifle, strode forward and scooped her up into his arms.

She heard his voice, low and angry. "Dear God, you're bleeding. Have you been shot?"

"No. At least, I don't think so." Strange. She couldn't feel anything except the heat where he was touching her. Suddenly, with his arms around her, cradling her to his chest, she felt warm and safe. All the fear she'd been holding back came rushing out in a deep sigh and a jumble of words. "I don't know why I'm bleeding. Maybe the branches..." Her words were halted by the sudden sting of tears. "I was so afraid.'' Without warning, tears streamed down her face in a torrent.

Like a child she wiped the back of her hand across her cheeks, leaving a bloody smear. Her voice was choked. "I don't know why I'm weeping. I never..."

With a muttered oath Wade carried her into the cabin, kicking the door shut behind him. In quick strides he crossed the room and laid her on his bed-roll spread out in front of a blazing fire.

Then he knelt beside her and examined her wounds. She was so small, so fragile. It tore at his heart to see her hurt.

Dipping his bandanna into a basin of water, he began to wash her, marveling at the delicate bones, the soft skin. Her flesh was torn and bloody, her gown, what was left of it, crisscrossed with snags and rips. Despite the amount of blood that smeared her arms and gown, he realized that all the cuts and scratches were superficial.

"If those men had found me—" she began.

"Shh." He placed a finger over her mouth to still her words. At the touch of her lips against his flesh he was as stunned as if he'd taken a blow. At once he pulled his hand away, making a great pretense of dipping his bandanna into the basin and wringing it out.

While he worked over her a wave of terrible anger rose up inside him, black and blinding. It hit him with the force of a blow that he was beginning to care far too much about this woman. The thought of Jade in the hands of a ruthless gang awakened feelings he neither wanted nor trusted.

She lay still as a wounded bird under his ministrations and marveled that such big hands could be so gentle.

He cleansed the deep wound in her arm, then tied a strip of clean linen around it. As he worked, his hand brushed her breast.

The flare of heat was instantaneous.

He glanced down and saw the color that flooded her cheeks. It was all the more obvious because of her pallor.

He strove to give no outward sign of his inner struggle as he wrapped her in his jacket. But his voice betrayed the strain as he muttered, "You'll be safe now."

A lie, he knew. In a way, she was no safer here with him than she would have been with that gang of outlaws.

She snuggled deep into the folds, feeling the warmth envelop her like a cocoon. With a sigh of contentment she said, "How did you happen to be here tonight?"

He ladled something from a pot over the fire. With his back to her, he said, "It was too late to head back to town, so I took refuge here. I was lucky to catch a couple of rabbits."

In one corner she could see the knife and discarded pelts. That would explain the knife and rifle, though she had never before seen Wade with a weapon. But as she glanced around, she noticed something else, as well. The narrow windows had been stuffed with rags, obscuring the view of the outdoors. But why? Was it to keep out the cold? Or could it be to prevent anyone passing by from seeing the light of the fire?

His reason for being here seemed logical enough. After all, hadn't they been caught unawares one other night? But this time the sky was clear and cloudless. And the town was probably only a few hours away.

Could he be avoiding someone? Why else would a man like Wade Weston prefer a rough shack to the comforts of Millie Potter's cozy boardinghouse?

Wade handed her a plate of stew and she sat up and ate, grateful to satisfy her hunger.

When she had eaten her fill he took the plate from her hand and offered her a steaming cup of coffee.

After only a couple of sips she returned the cup to him. "Thank you. You'll never know how grateful I am that you chose this night to be here."

He grew thoughtful as he refilled the cup from a blackened pot and sipped in silence.

Now that Jade was warm and safe and fed, it was too much effort to stay awake. But as she lay down and drifted on a cloud of contentment, several questions began to spin hazy clouds in her mind. If Wade Weston was truly a man of God, why was he so secretive? Who was he avoiding? Why, since he had already caught several rabbits for stew, was he still holding a rifle when she arrived? And why was he dressed in such strange garb?

Despite her troubling thoughts, or perhaps because of them, she tumbled into a shallow, fitful sleep.

Chapter Nine

Throughout the long night Wade forced himself to stay busy. He rubbed down Jade's lathered horse before turning it into the corral. After forking hay into the enclosure, he hauled several buckets of water from a nearby stream and poured them into a trough.

With rifle in hand he walked the nearby hills, keeping an eye out for intruders. He made half a dozen trips to the nearby woods, returning each time with his arms laden with firewood. By the time he'd finished, there was nearly a cord of wood stacked neatly beside the wall.

When he ran out of chores to occupy his time, he reluctantly returned to the little cabin. Straddling a rickety chair in one corner, he studied Jade as she slept.

She was so beautiful, so perfect, she might have been someone he'd imagined, just to satisfy an emptiness in his heart. But she was real. Far too real. And far too tempting.

God, he wanted to roll a smoke. He wanted a drink. He wanted . . . Jade.

He ran a hand through his hair in frustration. The last time they'd been alone in this cabin he'd had to fight an almost overpowering temptation. And he'd succeeded. But that was different. Tonight . . .

Why did she have to pick this night to return? To need him? To trust him?

Trust. He chided himself for such foolishness.

She sighed in her sleep and he felt the tightening in his loins.

Most of the time he had strength to spare. But tonight he'd just run out. He had demons of his own to fight tonight. And the presence of this woman was threatening to push him over the edge.

Her breathing became shallow and she began to murmur a few incoherent words. He realized that she was having a bad dream, reliving the fear of the chase.

"No . . . hide . . . find me."

He took a calming breath and knelt beside her, taking pains not to touch her. "Jade. Wake up," he said gently.

When she continued twisting and writhing, he had no choice but to touch a hand to her shoulder. He said more sharply, "Jade. Come on. Wake up. It's just a dream."

With a cry she sat up. The jacket slipped from her shoulders, revealing the torn sleeve, the gaping bod-

ice. For the moment she took no notice. But Wade
did. And felt his throat go dry at the sight of her.

Her hair, sleek and black as midnight, fell in dis-
array around a face that stirred him each time he
looked at it.

Fear made her eyes wide. She shrank from his
touch. "Who...? What...?" As realization dawned,
a long, deep sigh was wrenched from her. She leaned
forward, touching her cheek to his in an achingly
sweet gesture. "Oh, Wade. I thought for a moment..."

"I know." The touch of her cheek against his was
causing the most bittersweet agony of his life.

He brought his hands to her shoulders, intending
to hold her at arm's length. But one touch of her,
and all restraint vanished.

She was so incredibly sweet. And trusting. And he
needed to hold her. Just for a moment.

With great tenderness he stroked a hand along her
back. She sighed and leaned into him. It seemed the
most natural thing in the world to press his lips to her
temple and murmur words meant to soothe.

"It's all right." It had been a long time since he'd
felt this quickening of the pulse. "You're safe now."
As safe as any lamb in the clutches of a wolf, he be-
rated himself.

"I know. And I'm so grateful you're here." She
closed her eyes and absorbed his quiet strength. "If
you hadn't been here, I'd be alone and cold and
hungry. And afraid," she whispered. "So afraid."

"There's nothing to be afraid of now." Except for the vulture whispering all these sweet lies in your ear. He felt lower than a snake. And unable to stop himself.

She liked his arms around her. Liked being held against his chest, feeling the unsteady rhythm of his heartbeat. Unsteady? She realized it was. As erratic as her own. And thundering like a runaway stagecoach.

"I'm glad it will be morning soon. I was feeling so lost and frightened until I found you here. And I'm still a long way from home." She shivered and felt his arms tighten around her.

"I'll be right here with you. I'm not going anywhere." He framed her face and stared down into her eyes. The touch of her stripped his mind of all thought but one. He had to taste her. Now. His hands tangled in her hair, drawing her head back.

She could read the desire in his eyes. For a moment she stiffened. Then, just as quickly, she relented.

His lips nibbled hers and he filled himself with the sweet, exotic taste of her. The kiss was easy, gentle, giving her a chance to draw away. But she didn't. Couldn't. Not with the dark, mysterious flavor of him filling her senses, and the slow, drugging need for him beginning to stir.

"Jade." His voice was a sigh against her lips. "Tell me to stop."

"No. I . . ." Instead of drawing away, she leaned closer and brought her arms around his waist. Her fingertips encountered bare flesh where his shirt had tugged free. Her breath hitched in her throat. "I can't."

The moment she touched him, his arms tightened around her, drawing her firmly against the length of him.

"Neither can I."

Now there was nothing gentle or civilized about the kiss. His mouth savaged hers. With teeth and tongue and lips he plundered, giving her no time to think.

He'd known. Known that all the careful planning, the proper manners, the civility could be peeled away in one careless moment. That's why he had worked so hard to avoid this. To avoid her. But it no longer mattered. All that mattered was this. The heat. The power. The pleasure. The woman in his arms.

The need to touch her was too great. He ran a hand up her back, over her shoulder, along her throat.

She moved under his touch, arching herself like a cat with each stroke. If she were a cat, she'd be purring. His touch soothed her, eased her tension, brushed away her fears. Then, just as she began to relax, that same touch aroused, electrified, struck sparks.

"Wade. Hold me." Her body was alive with needs. Needs that had her responding to his kiss in a way she'd never dreamed possible.

Her hands clutched at the front of his shirt, drawing him closer.

"Kiss me."

With a little moan her lips opened to his probing tongue. She drank in the taste of him, dark and mysterious, and wanted more. When he took the kiss deeper, she sighed and moved in his arms, discovering needs she hadn't even known existed.

The moment his lips touched hers he was lost, caught up in a passion so unexpected, so unsettling, it startled him.

He knew he needed to back away. Now, before he crossed the line. But as he took the kiss deeper, all thought fled. All he could do was hold her, touch her, taste her, until he had his fill.

She tasted as exotic as she looked. Like a rare flower that grew in some secluded glade. Like a unique spice that remained on the tongue to tease, to tempt.

And all the while he continued to kiss her, and stroke her, until the heat rose up between them, making them half-mad with it.

The thought of stripping off her clothes and lying with him, flesh to flesh, had her breath coming harder, faster. With a sigh she gave herself up to the pleasure Wade was offering. Pleasure beyond anything she had ever known.

As his mouth continued to plunder hers, she forgot everything she'd ever learned about resisting a man's advances. All her tutoring, all her training had been in vain. All she could do was cling to him while his lips brought her pleasure beyond belief.

In some small corner of her mind she heard a sigh that spoke of passion, of gradually awakening desire. But she didn't recognize it as her own voice.

"I thought I could fight this. But I don't have the strength," he murmured against her throat. "I want you, Jade. And have since the first time I saw you."

He lifted his head and studied her in the light of the fire. Her lips were warm and moist and thoroughly kissed. Her eyes were heavy-lidded with passion. Her chest rose and fell with each labored breath.

"And I... I want..." She pursed her lips in a little pout when she saw the way he was staring at her.

Suddenly, without warning, he lifted a finger to her lips and traced their fullness, then dipped his finger into the moistness of her mouth. Next he lifted his finger to his own mouth and tasted her.

She froze at the flashback to her past.

This couldn't be happening.

He couldn't be...

She gasped. Her eyes rounded in shock and recognition. For a moment she felt as if all the air had been squeezed from her lungs. Then, finding her voice, she managed to say, "It was you."

At her words, he studied her through narrowed eyes.

"The voice that night was only a whisper. And your face was different. Heavily bearded like a mountain man. But I've never forgotten the way you kissed me on my sixteenth birthday. And the way you traced my lips, as though...tasting me."

After a lengthy silence he found his voice and reached for her. "You've mistaken me for someone else."

"No." She pushed free of his arms, feeling suddenly cold. With her breath coming hard and fast she looked at him, as if seeing him for the first time. "You were dressed all in black. You were gambling. And winning. Someone called you Nevada. And you killed a man. Calmly, without emotion. And then you kissed me."

When he said nothing in his own defense she scrambled to her feet and stalked across the room, needing to put some distance between them.

With her back to him she stared into the flames of the fire and said, "It's bad enough that you're a gambler and a gunman. But to make matters worse, you're a liar, as well." She turned and pinned him with a look of pure hatred. "The worst sort of liar, who passes himself off as a man of peace."

She felt tears sting her eyes and blinked them back. She wouldn't allow herself to cry over the shattered memory she had foolishly cherished all these years. The memory of her first kiss from a man who'd excited her. And fueled her dreams. Oh, such wonderful, fanciful dreams. "How could you do this? How could you lie to me?"

Because he still wanted to reach out to her, he curled his hands into fists at his sides. His voice was carefully controlled. "It isn't a lie. I am a man of peace. At least, I try to be. And I'll make no apology for the kiss. Then or now. As for honesty, Miss Jewel, if you were being honest, you'd have to admit that you returned my kisses." His lips curved into a bitter smile. "Then, and now."

Because it was the truth, and hit too close to home, she lifted her chin in that haughty manner he'd come to know so well. Fury turned her voice into a weapon as sharp, as cutting, as the blade at her waist. "At least now that I know what your game is, I have the decency to put an end to it. As for you, you have no decency at all. You lied to me. And you lied to the people of Hanging Tree. This is all some sort of cruel, heartless game to you, isn't it?"

"A game?"

Her mind raced. "Didn't you tell me that you had no intention of staying here? That these people meant nothing to you? For all I know, you could be using your charms to learn about the people of Hanging Tree, so you can take advantage of them. Just as you took advantage of me. Is that what you're planning?"

He had gone very still. The anger that simmered inside wasn't visible on his face, or in his voice when he spoke. "That isn't even worthy of a response." He glanced toward the closed door. "It'll be light soon. I'll see you home."

"You needn't bother. I can take care of myself."

He was across the room in quick strides, his hands closing over the tops of her arms in a painful grasp. "I said I'd see you home. After that, you'll never have to see me again."

Pain and anger made her careless. "That suits me just fine. The sight of you makes me sick. Now take your hands off me."

He should have released her. But his own anger got the better of him. "A minute ago you liked my hands on you. A minute ago you were wondering what it would feel like to indulge yourself in pleasures of the flesh with me."

There was a dangerous light in his eyes. A light that frightened yet excited her, causing her pulse rate to climb.

She hated him for having read her emotions so easily. Though she wanted to deny it, it would be a lie. She had wanted him. And still did, if truth be told.

"It isn't too late, Miss Jewel." His tone hardened. "You could find out right now. Right here. Would you like that? Would you like me to show you just how easy it would be? And just how pleasurable?"

Just as in San Francisco, Jade was both attracted to and repelled by the danger, the unknown. But to her credit, she kept her voice carefully controlled. "Let go of me."

He watched her eyes as he lowered his hands to his sides and took a step back. Her fear of him had faded, but not entirely. Though she kept her head high, her spine rigid, there was a wary, watchful expression in her eyes.

He should apologize for that last outburst. But he was still too furious. Instead he turned on his heel and headed for the door. "I'll get the horses."

Chapter Ten

Though dawn light streaked the eastern horizon, the sky was still awash in stars. Widow's Peak silhouetted against a backdrop of pearl light was a spectacular sight that never failed to stir the soul. But the two who viewed it this day took no notice.

They rode the entire distance in silence.

Jade didn't know which was worse—the cold fury in Wade's eyes or the extremely polite manners he exhibited.

He remained directly beside her the entire way. And yet he only looked at her when it was absolutely necessary. When her horse stumbled he reached a hand to steady her, then withdrew it immediately, as though the touch of her repelled him.

Her heart had never felt so heavy. Her mood had never been so blue. Reverend Wade Weston was a fraud, a cheat, a liar. And so was the handsome, mysterious gunman from her past whose memory had fueled her dreams. Everything he stood for was a lie.

She'd been a fool. A silly, childish fool. And she had no one to blame but herself. She had known, or rather sensed, that the gunman in the Golden Dragon had things to hide. Why else would he have disappeared without a trace, never to be seen in San Francisco again?

What better way for a gunman with a past to start a new life than to pose as a man of peace? Perhaps that was why she had never made the connection between Wade Weston and the mysterious gunman. Though both had stirred something inside her, they had seemed the extreme opposite of one another. To realize now that they were one and the same man . . .

In her mind the most shocking thing of all was that, regardless of his pose, he was the only man who had ever touched her. She had not only permitted it, she had encouraged it.

She had shamed her mother, who had taught her—for the success of her business—to hold herself aloof from all men. And she had shamed her father, who had always prided himself on being a fine judge of people. How could she have given her heart to a liar and a cheat?

As they paused on a hill overlooking the Jewel ranch, Jade broke her self-imposed silence. "I wish to ride the rest of the way alone."

"I said I'd see you safely home."

"No." Her eyes flashed a challenge. "If you're concerned for my safety, you can remain here until I reach the barn. But I don't want you to come any closer to my home."

He gave a curt nod. "As you wish, Miss Jewel."

She shot him an icy stare. "Is Wade Weston your real name? Or did you invent that, as well?"

His eyes were as hard as granite. "I thought you knew, Miss Jewel. Everything about me is phony." He touched a hand to the brim of his hat and wheeled his mount.

She remained where she was until he disappeared over a rise. Then, with a heavy heart, she turned her horse toward home.

Diamond, Pearl and Ruby came racing from the house when they spied her horse.

"Where have you been?" Diamond shouted.

"We were so worried," Pearl called before Jade could say a word, "when one of your horses returned without you!"

"The wranglers spent the night scouring the countryside, *chérie,*" Ruby scolded.

"I'm sorry. Truly sorry. Forgive me." As Jade slid from the horse, she told them about encountering the gang of outlaws, and how she had managed to outrun them.

"Another night with the good reverend," Ruby said with a sly laugh.

Jade's lips curved into a scowl. "And the last."

"What's wrong?" Diamond asked, sensing the underlying pain in her words. "What's happened?"

"Nothing," Jade said quickly. Too quickly. All three of her sisters were watching her closely. "Now, if you don't mind, I would like a bath and a chance to sleep in a bed."

As she hurried away, the three young women looked at one another in consternation. Something had happened to rob Jade of her usual sunny nature. But from the look in her eyes, she had no intention of sharing it with anyone.

"It was those murderous outlaws," Diamond said, checking the pistols in her holsters.

"Of course. That sort of fear would weigh heavily on anyone's mind," Pearl said with an emphatic nod.

Ruby clucked her tongue. "If you ask me, it is not the band of outlaws that causes Jade such unhappiness. It is something else. Or someone else."

Whatever it was, Jade kept it to herself. For the rest of the day she remained in her room, the door firmly locked. Even Carmelita's spiced chicken couldn't budge her from her isolation.

Late that night, as her three sisters started up the stairs to bed, she announced that she was leaving the following morning for San Francisco.

"This has all happened so quickly. I wish you'd reconsider." Diamond, dressed in her usual buckskins, stood between Pearl and Ruby, watching with dismay as the stagecoach driver loaded Jade's trunks.

As always, the presence of the Jewel sisters in the town of Hanging Tree drew a crowd of curious on-lookers.

Marshal Quent Regan sauntered from his office to pause in the dusty street. His deputy, Arlo Spitz, ambled out behind him, squinting in the afternoon sun. Several men, women and children wandered from Durfee's Mercantile to stop and watch. Lavinia Thurlong and Gladys Witherspoon pushed past everyone, hoping to catch a word or phrase of conversation.

"Looks like you're taking a trip," Lavinia called.

Jade merely nodded.

"Interesting," Gladys said with an arched brow. "I hear Reverend Weston's gone and left town, too. Told Millie Potter he didn't know when he'd be back."

The Jewel women stared at each other in consternation, then turned to Jade. But from the tight line of her lips, they knew she wasn't about to add to their store of knowledge on the subject of the good preacher.

The sisters, knowing every word would be repeated throughout the countryside, lowered their voices.

"I wish you'd stay," Diamond said stiffly.

"I told you." Jade drew Diamond close for a quick hug. "It's important that I see to my mother's business. She poured her life into the Golden Dragon. It's a valuable commodity. I must find a buyer for it."

"But you gave us no warning," Pearl complained. "And now you say you may be gone for weeks, or even months. Why now? And why must you stay away so long?" The young woman's usually smooth brow was furrowed with concern, especially now that she had heard about the reverend's leave-taking. There was something amiss here.

Jade squeezed her hand, then gathered her close and kissed her soft, pale cheek. "My building is nearing completion here in town. It will need to be furnished. There are things in the Golden Dragon in San Francisco that would be useful here. I must catalog the many treasures and consider each item very carefully before deciding which to keep and which will be sold. And then there are my employees. Once I've arranged for a broker to sell the building, I intend to arrange jobs for all who depend upon me."

"Promise you will be careful, *chérie*," Ruby whispered as she opened her arms for a tender embrace. "It is a long journey from here to San Francisco."

"I promise."

"It is not just the journey that concerns me," Ruby muttered for Jade's ears alone. "It is you and a certain...gentleman. I think there is much between you that you have not told us."

"Don't worry. I can take care of myself. As for the gentleman—" she sighed "—he doesn't deserve that title." She breathed in the heady perfume of the bayou that always seemed to surround this young woman. "I'll miss you, Ruby." She turned to the others. "I'll miss all of you."

The driver lashed the trunks to the top of the stage and climbed down. "We're ready to roll, Miss Jewel."

"Thank you." She placed a small hand in his and allowed him to help her into the stage. As he closed the door, she leaned out the window and caught her sisters' outstretched hands. "Don't worry about me. I'll return before you have time to miss me."

As the team leaned into the harness and the stage lurched ahead, Jade watched until the town of Hanging Tree had faded into the dust. Then she leaned back and closed her eyes, surprised by the prickle of tears behind her closed lids.

So, the truth had driven Wade away. She wouldn't cry, she told herself. There would be no tears shed over Wade Weston, or whatever his name was. Not now. Not ever. He was out of her life. For good.

"Welcome, Jade. You have been sorely missed."

"And you, Aunt Lily."

The slim, shapely woman with upswept blond hair and a fashionable beaded gown was not really a relative. The title was one of honor. Lily Austin had been Ahn Lin's most trusted assistant. It was Lily to whom Jade had turned when Ahn Lin had died. And it was Lily who had promised to keep the Golden Dragon running smoothly when Jade had rushed to Texas at the news of her father's death. When Jade had written a long, impassioned letter stating that she wished to remain in Texas to get to know her new family, Lily had understood. She would wait as long as necessary for Jade to decide the next step in her life's drama.

The door was closed by an Oriental giant whose body rippled with muscles honed through years of labor on the docks of San Francisco. The warrior, Lee Yin, had been chosen by Onyx Jewel himself to guard the women of Ahn Lin's business. His loyalty to Jade Jewel was unquestionable.

As the door closed, he leaned against it and watched as the party of women climbed the stairs.

In Jade's suite of rooms Lily settled herself on a lounge while two maids unpacked the bulging trunks. Jade moved restlessly around the luxurious rooms that had been her home for all of her life. She had no need to speak of the homesickness she had suffered. Her deep silence, broken only by an occasional sigh, spoke volumes.

She touched a hand to the silk wall coverings, the elegantly embroidered bed linens, the heavy velvet draperies at the windows. She opened the window wide and breathed deeply, filling her lungs with the scents that were uniquely San Francisco. These familiar sights and sounds would always touch her in a special way. The fine, misty rain that was so much a part of the city. The scents of ocean and harbor carried on the damp breeze. The streets littered with hand carts, horse-drawn carriages and a swell of humanity from every part of the world.

"Perhaps you would like to rest. We can talk later."

Jade seemed momentarily confused, as though surprised that the others were still here. Her mind was awhirl with memories. "Yes, please. It has been a long journey, and I am weary."

Lily clapped her hands. At once one of the maids approached, eyes downcast, head bowed. The bed linens were turned down. A second maid helped Jade to undress. Naked, she slid between rose-scented sheets. The draperies were drawn. By the time the door to her room was closed, and Lily and the maids had taken their leave, she was back in her childhood. Steeped in memory.

Jade lay in her bed listening to the sounds that filtered through the walls. During the past months she had learned to adjust to the sounds of life on a cattle ranch. Cattle lowing, wranglers swearing, hoofbeats thundering across hard-packed earth. Now, as darkness covered the land, she heard the music of the city. The music that had lulled her to sleep since her birth here in San Francisco. A foghorn sounded out in the bay, warning other boats of its presence. On the streets, carriages rolled past. Below stairs, the notes of a violin, high and pure, were a soothing background to the clink of glasses, the deep rumble of men's voices and the occasional trill of feminine laughter.

A door opened softly, then closed. The light of a lantern drew closer, illuminating the room. Jade sat up and watched as Aunt Lily approached and set the lantern on her night table.

"Do you wish a bath?" she asked.

"Yes, please."

Lily clapped her hands and two servants approached, balancing an ornate tub between them. Several more servants trailed behind, carrying buckets of steaming water. Soon a bath had been prepared in front of a cozy fire. With a sigh of contentment Jade settled into the water.

She had forgotten how wonderful it felt to be pampered. Her hair was washed and wrapped in a warm towel. Her body was soothed with oils and perfumes. By the time she stepped from the tub, she felt renewed and refreshed.

A maid approached holding several gowns.

"You will choose, please."

"This one." Jade chose her usual, a gown of shimmering green silk with a mandarin collar and black frog fasteners. When it was slipped over her head it skimmed the curves of her body like a second skin. She wondered if her Texas sisters had ever experienced the feel of silk against naked flesh, with no undergarments as barriers.

The narrow skirt was slit to the thigh on either side for ease of walking, revealing a length of shapely leg. On her feet she wore dainty green satin slippers. At her throat was her only jewelry—the rope of gold with the glittering onyx and jade. Each time she wore it, she felt her father's presence beside her.

For a moment she clutched it tightly in her fingers, savoring the memory of her birthday.

I feel you with me still, honorable Father. Here, in the place where you presented this to me, more than ever.

With a shake of her head she brought herself firmly back to the present.

She was led to a dressing table, where her hair was brushed and secured with jeweled combs so that it fell, sleek and smooth, over one breast.

She turned to study her reflection in the tall looking glass. Gone was the simple young woman who had arrived tired and dusty from the trail. In just a matter of hours she had reverted to the young woman who had been trained at her mother's knee to suit the sophisticated tastes of the men who frequented the Golden Dragon.

"Aunt Lily, I feel like a new woman."

"In fact, you look like the Jade I remember. Come," Lily said, holding out her hand. "We'll dine. And you'll tell me everything that has happened since you left. I especially want to hear about your father's home in Texas."

As she descended the stairs, Jade thrilled to the foreign languages, the many strange dialects. As she entered the formal parlor, she greeted the men in their own tongues, conversing easily in French, Spanish, Italian, German. As she moved on, their admiring glances followed her.

Lily led the way to a small alcove, where a table had been set with fine china and crystal.

When a servant poured wine, Jade lifted a brow. "Spirits?"

Lily smiled. "I know. We rarely indulge. But it is a special occasion."

Again Jade was reminded of another occasion. Without realizing it, she glanced around the room.

"Are you expecting company?" Lily asked.

Jade felt heat stain her cheeks. To cover her discomfort she said, "No. It's just that this is all so new, and yet so familiar. I shall miss this place."

"You talk as though you are leaving."

Jade waited until the servant walked away before saying, "I am." She caught Lily's hand between both of hers. "Aunt Lily, I have come to a painful decision. My home now is in Texas. I've come back to sell the Golden Dragon."

She could see the shock and horror her words caused. Lily's eyes widened. Her lips trembled, and she caught her lower lip between her teeth to keep from crying out.

"You cannot be serious." Lily pulled her hand free and lifted the crystal goblet to her lips, drinking deeply. "What will happen to all of us?"

"I...was hoping you would come with me. I have already begun to duplicate the Golden Dragon in my new home."

Lily gave an incredulous laugh. "You want me to live in Texas? In the dusty little town of... What is it called? Hanging Tree?"

Hearing it from Lily's lips made it sound so impossible. And yet, until this moment, she had truly believed she could succeed in her dream.

Jade sipped her wine and chose her words carefully. "I have found family in Texas. Sisters." Over dinner she described the three young women with whom she now shared her life. "Diamond and Pearl have married, and now have homes of their own. Diamond's ranch adjoins ours, and Pearl's home is actually on our land, just across Poison Creek."

Lily cringed. "Is the water poisoned?"

Jade stifled her laugh. After all, she had once wondered the same thing. "The water is as pure as a mountain stream." She shrugged. "Who knows where such names come from? Anyway, Ruby and I are still living in Father's ranch house, but we manage to see Diamond and Pearl every day. We've become a family. A true family. And I do not wish to be separated from them. But I must have a purpose in my new life in Texas. And the only thing I know is this."

Lily set down her fork. She had managed a few bites, but the food now stuck in her throat. As did the regret.

Lifting her goblet, she sipped before saying as gently as she could manage, "I understand your need for family. Each time your father left, I could see the pain in your eyes. But I always thought we were your family. All of us here, who have worked at the Golden Dragon."

"You know I love you." Jade's eyes were troubled. "And you have always been an important part of my life. I want you to continue to share my life. But Diamond, Pearl and Ruby are my father's daughters. We have just now found each other. I cannot bear the thought of being separated from them. There is so much they can tell me about my father's life when he was not with me."

Lily studied her young friend. With a wan smile she pushed away from the table. "I will need some time to ponder this. In the meantime, I have work to do." She held out a hand. "Will you join me?"

Jade nodded and accepted her hand.

Soon both women were moving through the rooms, stopping occasionally to talk, to listen, to summon a waiter or smooth over a misunderstanding.

Leaving Lily to chat with a group of gentlemen, Jade continued to move through the public rooms until she came to the private parlor where Lily had informed her a high-stakes poker game was in progress.

Jade swept into the room, then closed the door with a soft click. A pall of rich cigar smoke hung over the table. The voices were subdued, except for an occasional curse as the cards were dealt. She smiled at the young woman who was seated at the head of the table, dealing. Her smile was still in place as her gaze scanned the half-dozen men, several of whom had women standing behind them, lighting their cigars or silently watching the game.

Suddenly her smile froze. She felt her breath catch in her throat.

A man dressed all in black looked up. His face was heavily bearded and his clothes still bore the dust of the trail. But there was no mistaking those strange, tawny eyes that seemed to see clear through her. Or the daunting curve of those lips as he scowled before returning his attention to the cards, effectively dismissing her.

It was Wade Weston. And yet not Wade.

He more nearly resembled, in fact, the mysterious gunman from her past.

Chapter Eleven

For the space of several seconds Jade was forced to grip the back of a chair while she struggled to compose herself. Then, on legs that felt like rubber, she made her way around the table, greeting several of the men she knew.

"Jade, my dear," said a courtly gentleman. "We've missed you. I hear you've been in Texas. My condolences on the death of your father."

"Thank you, Senator Hammond. It is good to be back in San Francisco."

"Gentlemen," the senator said to the others at the table, "may I present Miss Jade Jewel. This lovely lady is the owner of the Golden Dragon."

As they started to get to their feet she waved a hand. "Please. I would not want to interrupt your game."

"But this is the most pleasant of interruptions, my dear." The senator indicated the players. "Jade, I'd like you to meet Elmer Miller, owner of Miller Mining. And this is Christopher Hawley, who owns San Francisco's finest carriage works."

Throughout the introductions Jade managed to smile and nod at all the appropriate times. And though she appeared charming and relaxed, her mind was in a turmoil.

"And this is one of the finest gamblers I've ever had the good fortune to oppose," the senator said with a trace of affection. "May I present Nevada."

"Miss Jewel." Wade bowed his head slightly in acknowledgment, and continued to meet her unflinching gaze.

Jade could read nothing in his eyes. They were as cool and clear as amber glass.

In truth, he was as stunned as she. The last he'd seen of her, she'd been riding toward her ranch house. He'd had no reason to think she would leave Texas. He felt a sudden burst of anger. What in hell was she doing here in San Francisco? And why did it have to be now? With a supreme effort he managed to bank his temper.

"May I buy you a bit of sherry later, my dear?" the senator asked, brushing a kiss to her cheek.

Jade nodded. "Thank you. Lily will find me when you've finished here." To the others she said, "I wish you all good luck, gentlemen. May the cards be kind to you."

She turned toward the door and forced herself to walk slowly, even though her first inclination was to bolt and run. She could feel Wade's dark gaze burning into her back until the door closed behind her.

Once she was safely in her office, and away from prying eyes, she sank into a chair behind her desk and clasped her hands together tightly.

Wade Weston. Here in San Francisco. So this was why he had left Hanging Tree so abruptly. He'd had a sudden desire to return to his old habits. But he was no longer the small-town preacher, Wade Weston. He was the gambler, Nevada.

There was nothing left of the gentle man she had known in Texas. From the pistols at his hips to the tumbler of whiskey at his elbow he was giving notice that he was every inch the mysterious gunman.

What was she to do? She pressed her hands to her face in a gesture of defeat. Oh, what was she to do now? How would she get through the days and weeks to come, with the knowledge that her dream lover was here in the flesh? And that the old dream had become a nightmare?

The piano was silent. In the public rooms the voices had faded. In the small hours of the morning the Golden Dragon had grown quiet, except for an occasional trill of laughter, or a creak on the stairs.

Senator Hammond, having lost a considerable fortune, had sought out Jade. The two old friends had shared a few fond memories of her parents over a glass of sherry before he'd taken his leave. The game had ended, the players scattered. Some had gone home. Others had moved on to other pleasures. And those women who were not otherwise occupied had gone to sleep.

Though her heart wasn't in it, Jade doggedly continued going over the ledgers. It was better than giving in to the weariness that held her in its grip. And infinitely better than facing her old, empty bedroom.

The door to her office suddenly opened. When she looked up, she was surprised to see the man who had been dominating all her thoughts. He strode casually across the room until he reached her desk.

He was as handsome and mysterious as she remembered. And her reaction was the same: her heart beat wildly, her palms grew moist, her throat felt dry as dust.

But instead of pleasure at the sight of him, she felt a deep welling of fear and anger. Fear because she knew how attracted she was—an attraction she was determined to fight. Anger that she could feel such things for a liar and a cheat.

Of the two she much preferred anger. It was an emotion she could deal with. She let the anger take over.

"A gentleman always knocks before entering a lady's room."

"I'm sure he does." He opened a box on her desk and helped himself to a cigar, then held a match to the tip. Sitting on her desk, he leaned back, a wreath of rich smoke curling over his head. On his finger was a ring of twisted gold, with an amber stone that caught and reflected the light. With a smile he added, "But nobody ever accused Nevada of being a gentleman."

"What are you doing here in San Francisco?" she demanded.

"I might ask you the same thing."

"I have every right to be here. Have you forgotten that I own this place?"

"I've forgotten nothing." He shot her a meaningful glance and was rewarded with a sudden flush to her cheeks.

He stretched out his long legs in a relaxed pose.

She had the impression that he was as relaxed as a panther on the prowl.

"My money helped build the Golden Dragon, Miss Jewel."

"That doesn't give you the right to barge in to my private office."

He merely smiled. "It doesn't give me any rights at all. But then, I never needed permission to do as I pleased."

She got to her feet, her back rigid, her chin high. "Do as you please somewhere else. I don't want you here in the Golden Dragon."

"Don't you?" He set the cigar in a crystal ashtray, then crossed the room and poured himself a glass of brandy from a decanter. As an afterthought he asked, "Would you care to join me?"

She shook her head in refusal.

He downed the drink in one long swallow, then poured a second, carried it back to her desk and sat down again. "I'll remind you, Miss Jewel, that I brought you a great deal of business tonight. The Golden Dragon's cut of the jackpot was worth nearly ten thousand dollars."

It galled her to admit that he was right. Lily had been ecstatic about the sudden influx of gamblers when Nevada had arrived on the scene. She'd boasted that the man was a magnet for all the wealthy players in San Francisco.

Instead of acknowledging it, Jade merely glared at him. "Am I supposed to be grateful?"

"I hope so. And if you'd like to show your appreciation in some...special way, you won't hear me object." The look he gave her had her cheeks flaming.

He seemed to be actually enjoying the role of gambler and gunman. Or was this his true self, and the preacher merely a pose? "How can you be so contemptible?"

"I've had a lot of practice." He sipped his brandy and nodded toward the pile of cash on her desk. "That money should pay a few bills."

"And what about you?" she demanded. "Did you win or lose?"

"I made considerably more than the Golden Dragon, Miss Jewel. I'm a very lucky gambler."

"So I've heard." She rounded the desk, intent upon ending their discussion. But as she swept past him his hand snaked out, catching her roughly by the wrist.

"Going somewhere?" He was on his feet and dragging her so close she could feel the heat of his breath against her cheek.

"It's late. I'm going to bed. I suggest you do the same."

"It would be my pleasure. Your room or mine?"

"I sleep alone."

"I'd be happy to change that."

She stared down at his offending hand. "Let me go."

"And if I don't?"

He could almost see the sparks coming from those dark eyes. "If you don't release me at once, I'll be forced to summon Lee Yin."

He knew the giant would have no hesitation about snapping his bones like twigs. The Asian had removed many a careless gunman from the Golden Dragon. And his loyalty to Jade was unquestioned.

"I wouldn't do that if I were you."

"And why not?"

"I'd have the blood of an innocent man on my conscience."

"I didn't think the gambler Nevada had a conscience."

"He doesn't."

She deliberately kept her tone harsh, to hide the pain she felt. "What happened to Reverend Wade Weston, the preacher of Hanging Tree?"

His voice was a low growl of anger. "He doesn't exist any longer. He outlived his usefulness."

She felt the strength in the hand holding her and experienced a tremor of alarm. "I'm truly sorry to hear that. I liked him. At least, I liked him more than the gambler Nevada."

"Really? I should think you'd be relieved. Have you forgotten that in Hanging Tree the Reverend Weston would have to stand with the people who oppose you?"

"At least you would stand for something. As far as I can see, the gambler Nevada stands for nothing. Except his own selfish pleasures."

"Speaking of which..." He smiled suggestively, and she felt her heart turn over in her chest. How was it that one man's dangerous smile had such power over her emotions?

She used what she hoped was her most commanding tone. "I want you to leave. Now."

He drew her fractionally closer, his eyes never leaving hers. "No, you don't. What you really want is the same thing I want. A chance to finish this thing between us."

She wanted desperately to deny it. But she knew he spoke the truth. And it shamed her deeply. "There can be nothing between us. Not now. Not ever."

"Then you won't mind if we share one last kiss. For old times' sake."

The brush of his lips on hers was so achingly sweet, she couldn't move. Her hands, poised to push him away, stilled their movements. Her body stiffened, then seemed to melt into him. He continued to keep the kiss light, the merest brushing of mouth to mouth. It was so tender, she thought her heart would break. It was everything she remembered from that first time, when she was sixteen and he was a mysterious, romantic stranger.

He lifted his head and stared down into her eyes. Eyes wide and unblinking. Eyes that told him she was as moved as he by what they had just shared.

"And now we know," he whispered.

Then, as if by mutual consent, they came together in a kiss so hot, so hungry, it threatened to engulf them in flames.

"By God, now we know." His voice was husky with feeling as his arms came around her, pinning her to the length of him.

With her head swimming, she clung to him as he backed her up until they were pressed against the wall. And still he dived into her, his lips and tongue taking her higher, his body imprinting itself on every part of hers.

Now there was no tenderness. Now there was only fire and passion and a force as volatile as the unleashed fury of a thunderstorm. His hands stroked, eager to touch, to learn. And his mouth devoured, wanting more, demanding all.

And she gave. Though she had never before known such demand, such desperate need, she gave without resistance. And wanted. Sweet heaven, how she wanted. The hunger was so deep, so gnawing, she felt consumed by it.

He knew he was taking her too far, too fast. But there was no way to stop it. The minute his lips had touched hers, he was lost. Lost in a blinding haze of need, a blaze of desire that he was helpless to quench.

He went on kissing her, denying the knowledge that pulsed with each lingering moment. Given her youth and inexperience, she had no wiles with which to fight him. He knew he was taking advantage of her. And it wasn't the way he'd wanted it. But he was beyond caring now. Driven by passion that was out of control, he could only take. And demand even more.

Jade's heart was pounding so loudly, she could hear it drumming in her ears.

Suddenly the pounding increased and she realized it wasn't just her heart. Someone was knocking on the door.

"Jade." The door was thrown open. "I thought..."

At the sound of Lily's voice, Nevada's head came up sharply.

The older woman took in the scene, her gaze lingering on the high color that painted Jade's cheeks, and the volatile emotions that clouded the gambler's eyes.

"Forgive me. I didn't realize..." She took a step back. "I thought you were alone."

Jade dragged air into her lungs and pushed herself free of the arms that held her. With each step she took away from him, her sanity returned. And with it, her firm resolve, which had been temporarily forgotten.

Seeing Lily about to retreat, she said, "There's no need to go. Nevada was just leaving. Weren't you?" She shot him a challenging look, daring him to argue.

Seeing it, he gave a grim smile. As he moved past her, he lifted a hand to smooth a tumble of her hair. At once she felt the rush of heat.

To cover her emotions she said, "What did you want, Aunt Lily?"

"It was nothing important. I was going to discuss business before accompanying you upstairs. But now I will see our guest to his room instead."

The older woman waited until Nevada moved past her. Then, with one last look of concern at Jade, she pulled the door closed and summoned Lee Yin.

The Oriental had been standing guard outside at the Golden Dragon's main door. No one broke the silence as the three walked along the darkened hall and climbed the stairs to the guest rooms.

When they reached Nevada's door, Lee Yin pulled it open and stood aside, arms crossed over his chest, his eyes watching warily. Nevada started inside, but Lily stopped him with a hand on his sleeve.

Her voice was low, for his ears alone. "I am surprised at you, Nevada. Those who have faced you in cards consider you a man of honor."

"What's your point, Lily?" Even now he found it difficult to speak. His voice was still raw with emotion.

Her tone softened. "Could you not see that Jade is an innocent?"

He met Lily's eyes. Though he cursed her timing, he realized that she had saved him from making a terrible mistake. He must have been crazed. He'd nearly done something they would both regret in the light of day.

"I won't forget it again," he muttered.

"See that you don't." She stepped back.

As he closed the door, he saw Lee Yin take up a position outside his room. And knew that if he were to attempt to leave before the night ended, he would be forced to taste the giant's wrath.

At least for another night, Jade Jewel was safe.

He wondered if she felt as miserable as he.

Chapter Twelve

Lily paused to whisper in Jade's ear, "Nevada is back."

Jade looked up from the cluster of gentlemen in time to see a broad, muscled back disappearing into the game room. "That makes seven nights in a row," she commented. Then, realizing what she'd revealed, she snapped, "As if I care."

She saw the smile on Lily's lips, and it only deepened her resolve to ignore him.

Nevada had returned each night to indulge in high-stakes poker games, which sometimes lasted throughout the night and far into the morning.

The women of the Golden Dragon were charmed by him. And the men made it plain that they enjoyed his company.

Though Jade did nothing more than offer a perfunctory greeting, she couldn't help being aware of him. Even in a crowded room her gaze was drawn to him. No longer was he the unkempt trail rider. Now, like the others who frequented the opulent pleasure palace, he wore exquisitely tailored suits and starched white shirts with monogrammed cuffs. His wild mane of hair had been shorn, his face clean shaven.

Without a word he could touch her.

Now, as she entered the game room and moved among the players, she was aware of the dangerous look in his eyes. And of his long, slender fingers as he picked up the cards. Aware, too, of the way he watched her over the rim of his glass, or through the haze of his cigar smoke.

She greeted him with the same quiet reserve she used for all the players, with the exception of Senator Hammond, who brought a bright smile to her lips.

"Jade," the dealer said, "I don't believe you've met Virgil Trent."

"Mr. Trent. Welcome to the Golden Dragon."

"Some welcome." The gambler, who sat to the right of Nevada, was dressed in formal black frock coat and satin vest. The pile of chips in front of him was slowly dwindling.

He had demanded that a tumbler of whiskey be kept filled at all times. Each time the cards were shuffled, he drained the tumbler and watched through narrowed eyes while it was refilled.

Though he appeared to be no more than twenty, his eyes were cold and vacant, his mouth a grim, tight line of anger. "I've had better luck in a run-down saloon in Deadwood," he muttered.

"Then perhaps you would prefer to try your luck at some other game," Jade suggested.

"Only if you're the prize." His gaze raked her as he held out a fistful of money. "Name your price."

Lee Yin started across the room, ready to defend Jade's honor. But she immediately smoothed things over by saying lightly, "I had in mind faro, Mr. Trent. Or perhaps dice."

He glanced at the lady, and then at her bodyguard. "My game is poker. That is, when the players are clean."

"Are you suggesting that we cheat?" The senator's eyes flashed a challenge.

Virgil merely shrugged. "If the shoe fits..."

"More brandy, Senator Hammond?" Jade said softly.

The older man took a long breath, then turned his head to look at her. Seeing the pleading look in her eyes, he muttered, "Yes. Thank you, my dear."

Gradually the game commenced. Lee Yin returned to his position near the door.

The senator glanced across the table at Nevada. "This time I have you, my friend. I don't think you can beat three aces."

Nevada tossed down his cards and lifted his glass in a salute as the senator's hands closed around the pile of chips.

"I believe that's the first hand I've won tonight," Senator Hammond remarked as two of the players, tired of losing and offended by Virgil Trent's comments, pushed away from the table and left in disgust.

"And the last," Nevada put in, to everyone's laughter. Everyone except Virgil, who continued to remain silent, his eyes narrowed in thought.

As the cards were shuffled and dealt, Nevada watched Jade lean close to one of the players and hold a match to his cigar. Her presence was a distraction. A most pleasant one, but a distraction all the same. He enjoyed the way she moved, the exotic fragrance that whispered on the air as she passed by, and especially the way she colored whenever she happened to look his way.

Beside him, Virgil also took notice of the lady. Nevada's frown deepened.

"Are you in?" the dealer asked.

Nevada returned his attention to the cards. But though he won the next three hands, he seemed to derive no satisfaction from it.

Another player strolled away, leaving only the three men at the table.

While the dealer shuffled, Nevada took the time to study Jade. The nearness of her was far too unsettling. He'd been very careful to keep his distance, so that he never had the occasion to repeat that little scene in her office. Now that he'd had time to think it through, he realized that Lily was right. Jade was an innocent. And though she'd been groomed to take over her mother's business, and claimed to know all about satisfying men's needs, she had no firsthand knowledge. She knew only what had been passed on to her by her tutors.

It gave him a strange sense of satisfaction to know that. And yet, it was dangerous for a woman in her position. Though the men who passed through these doors abided by the rules and respected her as the owner of the establishment, there were some who would always want the forbidden. The more she held herself aloof, the more they would desire her.

He was honest enough to admit that he was first among them. He wanted her. And had, since the first time he'd seen her. As Reverend Wade Weston, the desire had been a difficult temptation to overcome. Now that he had resumed the role of the gambler Nevada, she had become an all-consuming fire in his blood. A fire that threatened to destroy them both.

"Where is your mind, my friend?" the senator asked sharply. "You've driven away most everyone else. I only remained because I figured sooner or later I would have to win another hand. Let's see if you can beat a pair of ladies." He dropped his cards, showing queens.

"Sorry." Nevada lowered his own hand, revealing three deuces.

When he raked in yet another jackpot, he met the stares of the senator and the dealer with a wry smile. "I guess it's just my night for winning."

"And mine for losing." Virgil Trent threw in his hand in disgust and pushed away from the table. He strode from the room, loudly demanding a drink.

Lily sent a young woman scrambling to see to his request.

"My thoughts, as well. I've contributed enough to your purse for one night," the senator said with a sigh. "I have no intention of giving you the shirt off my back, too."

He offered his hand and Nevada accepted. While the dealer tallied the chips and counted out the cash, the two men crossed the room to stand in front of the fireplace. Jade approached with tumblers of whiskey.

"I see the cards were good to you," she said as Nevada took the glass from her hand. Their fingers brushed and she looked up to find him watching her closely.

"I'm used to winning some and losing some," he muttered.

"And you, Senator." She offered him a drink. "I was sorry to hear that the cards were unkind to you tonight."

"It's not the first time, my dear. Nor will it be the last. Lady Luck is such a fickle creature. And tonight she chose to smile upon my friend here." He clamped an arm around Nevada's shoulders and the two men shared a smile.

"Jade, will you stay and have a drink with us?" the senator urged.

She shook her head. "Duty calls. Perhaps another time."

When she walked away, Nevada was unaware of the way his gaze followed.

Senator Hammond's voice beside him was a low rumble of laughter. "You'd better watch it, son. If Lee Yin sees that look in your eyes, he'll kill you just on principle."

Nevada swung his gaze toward the senator, arching a brow.

"I'm an old hand at reading men's eyes." The older man smiled. "And right now, son, yours are a dead giveaway. Oh, I don't blame you," he added hastily. "Jade is a rare beauty. But she's strictly off-limits."

"So I've been told." Nevada pulled himself back from his thoughts and offered his hand. "Thanks again for your contribution, Senator. I hope I'll see you tomorrow night."

"I wouldn't miss it. And now I have other pleasures in mind," the older man muttered before going off in search of Lily.

Nevada drained yet another tumbler of whiskey and stared broodingly into the flames. Though the hour was late and he was weary, he couldn't bring himself to leave.

"You seem troubled, Nevada."

At Lily's voice, his head came up. "Just... thinking."

"I ordered several of my women to inquire about your comfort. You sent them away," she said accusingly.

"Sorry. I'm not interested."

From across the room he could hear Jade's voice, conversing in fluent French. From his travels around the West, he'd mastered a smattering of languages. He recognized enough words to know that she was telling an amusing story. When she concluded, several gentlemen gave her admiring glances as she moved on.

"Your interest seems to lie in one particular woman," Lily remarked.

He looked away. "I'm a gambler, Lily. The only thing that interests me is the lure of the cards."

"I think you are trying to convince yourself of that," she said softly.

Across the room Jade held a flame to the tip of a man's cigar. Nevada let the sound of her laughter, low and deep, wash over him.

Beside him Lily stared pointedly at his hands, clenched tightly by his sides. "But you are not doing a very good job," she whispered.

Very carefully he unclenched his hands. He was feeling absolutely miserable. He'd come to a decision. It was time to move on, before this obsession with Jade Jewel got out of control. "It's late. I have things to do."

He turned to take his leave. Out of the corner of his eye he saw Virgil Trent forge a deliberate path through the crowded room toward Jade. When he reached her side he draped his arm around her shoulder and drew her close to murmur something in her ear. With a look of revulsion she tried to push him away. He gave a cruel sneer and tightened his grasp. She let out a cry.

At once Lee Yin began lumbering across the room. Just as he reached for Virgil, a shot rang out. The Asian giant seemed to stiffen, then he went down on one knee. Even as blood spurted from his wound, he lifted his arms, trying vainly to catch hold of the villain's throat. Virgil's booted foot in his groin sent him sprawling helplessly.

Jade gave a piercing scream until Virgil's hand covered her mouth, silencing her.

Most of the men in the room carried weapons. But as their hands went to their holsters, Virgil brought his pistol to his captive's temple. "Put your hands where I can see them," he shouted. "Any man who draws a gun will have this lady's blood on his hands."

When the men didn't move quickly enough, he took aim at a crystal chandelier and let loose with a volley of gunfire. Shards of glass rained down upon the people as women shrieked in terror and men lifted their hands in the air.

"Everyone down on the floor!" Virgil shouted.

Sobbing, whimpering, the women lay, covering their heads to protect themselves from further debris. The air was blue with curses as the men dropped to their knees.

Except for the sound of several women weeping, the crowded room fell deathly quiet.

"That's better," Virgil said. "Now stay where you are till I leave. I'm in a hurry to get the lady away from here."

"Where are you taking her?" Lily demanded.

"Someplace where we can be alone." He laughed, a high, shrill sound that scraped across nerves already strung as tightly as bowstrings. He glanced around in triumph. "Don't look so sad, ladies and gentlemen. After all, this is a house of pleasure. I'm just doing what any red-blooded Californian would do. Only I don't want any cheap whores. I prefer the madam herself. And I'm going to have my fun without paying for it."

"That's where you're wrong." Nevada's tone was calm and steady as he stepped through a doorway directly in front of the gunman, blocking his path. In his hand was his six-shooter. "This is about to cost you dearly, Trent."

For a moment Virgil froze, seeing the gun pointed at his chest. But it was the look in Nevada's eyes that had him sweating. It was the cool, deadly look of a seasoned killer.

Virgil tightened his grasp on Jade and jammed his pistol against her temple. "Maybe you weren't listening. I said I'd blow her away if any man drew a gun."

"Oh, I was listening. And I decided to call your bluff." Nevada took a step closer, until he could taste the stranger's fear.

He forced himself not to look at Jade. For to look at her, he would be reminded of all he was risking. He couldn't afford to lose his edge now. Instead, he stared directly into the gunman's eyes until he detected the flicker of fear.

It was all he needed. His tone was deceptively soft as he said, "I've just run out of patience, Trent. Either you drop your weapon and release the lady or you'll never see another sunrise. Or bed another woman."

"You're bluffing." A trickle of sweat beaded Virgil's forehead and began to run down the side of his face.

"There's one way to find out."

Virgil glanced around, seeking an escape. But the man in front of him blocked the only exit. His voice rose to a shrill chant. "If I can't have her, nobody can."

What happened next had everyone gasping. Virgil's finger tightened on the trigger of his gun, alerting Nevada to the fact that he was prepared to make good his threat. In the blink of an eye, before he could fire, Nevada's hand snaked out, yanking Jade free and shoving her roughly to the floor, out of the range of the bullet. There was a tremendous explosion of sound as both guns fired simultaneously.

For what seemed an eternity the two men stood facing each other, their faces twisted into masks of fury. Then, like a puppet dancing slowly on a string, Virgil's hand relaxed and his gun fell to the floor. His eyes widened in surprise as he sank to his knees, then slumped facedown.

Chaos erupted as the crowd got to its feet and began to surge forward. But suddenly they fell back as Nevada turned and they caught sight of him. Blood spilled from his chest, soaking the front of his shirt. The hand grasping the pistol dropped to his side. His face was ashen, his features contorted with pain.

"Like I said," he managed to gasp between clenched teeth, "this is my night for winning."

It was clear that he was gravely wounded. It was only by sheer force of will that he was still standing.

Chapter Thirteen

"Help me!" Jade's voice shattered the stunned silence as she caught Nevada by the arm before he could sink to the floor.

Several of the men hurried forward and urged him down onto a sofa.

Too weak to argue, he gritted his teeth against the pain. His eyes closed as he felt his life's blood slowly ebb.

"Let me have a look at him. I'm a doctor," came a voice close by.

But though Nevada could feel fingers probing and voices fading in and out of his consciousness, he couldn't seem to rouse himself enough to open his eyes.

"Forget about me," he whispered. "See to Lee Yin."

"The Oriental will live," came the same deep voice. "It's just a superficial wound. The man you shot, however, is dead. And you're going to join him, my friend, unless you put up the fight of your life.''

Nevada had been carried up the stairs to Jade's suite. The crowd had been dispersed. Only Jade, Lily and the doctor remained.

A hushed, breathless silence hung over the room, punctuated by the shallow breathing of the man on the bed.

Outside in the hallway, the women of the house milled about, speaking in whispers, peering intently through the partially open door as the drama unfolded.

The flicker of lantern light made eerie patterns on the walls and ceiling as the doctor's hands moved through an intricate dance of cutting, probing, tying, sponging.

A clock ticked on the mantel. It could have been hours, or mere minutes. Jade had lost all sense of time and place. She knew only that this man had given no thought to his own life while saving hers. She would do no less.

She had been taught since infancy to bear all of life's burdens stoically. But though she calmly assisted the doctor, handing him instruments, tearing strips of linen, her mind was in turmoil. She had been forced to accept the deaths of her beloved parents. Would she now have to face the death of the only man she'd ever loved?

Love. She was so stunned by the thought she could hardly breathe. How could she love a gunman? Especially one who had lied to her? Whose whole life had been a lie?

And yet, try as she might to deny it, she knew it to be true. Though it was completely illogical, she loved this man who hovered between life and death. Loved him as she would never love another man. He had broken through her wall of reserve. Had pierced the armor of her heart and claimed it for his own. And though she had fought to ignore him, had intended never to see him again, he had won.

"Jade?"

At the sound of her name she looked up in confusion.

Lily said gently, "The doctor needs more linen."

"Yes. Of course." She handed the dressings to the doctor and watched as he bound Nevada's wounds.

"Is he..." Lily glanced at Jade and spoke the question she knew was in her young friend's heart. "Will he live, doctor?"

"That's up to a higher power than mine, Lily," he said matter-of-factly. "I've done all I can." He turned to Jade. "I'd advise you to have someone remain with him throughout the night." He began to return his instruments to his bag. "The chloroform will keep him still for a while longer. But after that the pain will rouse him. When that happens, you may have to restrain him, for his own good."

"Is there anything I can give him for the pain?" she asked.

He handed her a packet. "This powder may help some. But I'm afraid he's going to have to suffer. That is, if he survives the night."

Seeing the worry etched on her brow, he touched a hand to her shoulder. "He has youth and strength on his side, my dear. That should count for something. And if his will to live is strong enough..." He shrugged expressively. "The next twenty-four hours will tell the tale."

Lily escorted him to the door. When she returned, Jade was seated in a chair beside the bed, her gaze riveted on the figure beneath the blankets, his hand held firmly between both of hers.

"You have to rest," Lily said. "I'll get one of the women to stay with Nevada."

"No." Jade waved her aside. "I can't think about sleep." She lifted anguished eyes. "Don't you see? He's my responsibility. If it weren't for me, he wouldn't be here, fighting for every breath."

"Jade, you'll make yourself ill. At least get out of those bloodstained clothes and rest for a little while."

"Leave me. I'll summon you if I need you." The young woman turned her head away, and Lily was forced to admit defeat. She had seen that stubborn look in her friend's eyes since she was a child. Jade's mind was made up. There would be no arguing with her now.

* * *

This was the hardest part, Jade thought. The waiting. And hoping. And praying. The long hours of the night seemed endless, the task before her daunting.

Each time Nevada's chest rose, then fell, she found herself willing him another breath, another moment of life. At times his breathing was so shallow it appeared to have ceased altogether. At other times it was labored, as though he had climbed to the very top of a mountain.

There was no flicker of feeling in his expression. Neither pain nor ease. His skin had taken on a sickly pallor. The big hand sandwiched between both of hers was cold, lifeless. Occasionally she brought it to her lips, or pressed it to her heart, but he gave no indication that he was even aware of her presence. He had slipped to some other place, beyond this world. Beyond her reach.

"Oh, Nevada," she murmured. "You were so brave, so bold. Please don't give up now. Stay with me. Please stay." Tears filled her eyes and coursed down her cheeks, but she took no notice as she brought her lips close to his ear and whispered, "Don't leave me, Nevada. I couldn't bear to lose you, too. I need you here with me."

She thought she felt his hand move in hers. At once she pulled a little away to look down at him. The expression on his face hadn't altered. And his hand still rested limply in hers. But his heart continued to beat. And his breathing, though shallow, was an indication that he was still fighting to live.

"I won't let you go," she muttered, linking her fingers with his. "Not without a fight."

Jade's head nodded and she jerked awake. Rubbing her stiff neck, she sat up straighter.

Someone had draped a blanket around her shoulders. A fresh log burned brightly on the hearth.

Her gaze flew to the figure in the bed. For a moment her breath caught in her throat. He was so still.

She leaned close and touched a finger to his throat. There was a pulse beat. Feeble. Thready. But at least he was still alive.

With a sigh she caught his hand between both of hers and lifted it to her lips. "The doctor was wrong," she murmured. "He said the pain would rouse you. Instead I feel you slipping away. Why can't you hear me?"

Her lids squeezed tightly shut against the pain. A tear slid from the corner of her eye and made its way to her jaw.

Suddenly she felt the touch of a fingertip, as gentle as the wings of a butterfly. Her lids snapped open. Dark eyes stared into cool green-gold ones.

"Why...are...you...crying?" He couldn't believe how hard it was to speak. Each simple word was like a knife-thrust deep in his chest.

"Nevada." His name was torn from her lips. "You're alive. Oh, you're alive."

Without a thought to what she was doing, she climbed into the bed and threw her arms around him in a fierce embrace.

Pain crashed through him and he had to fight a wave of dizziness. But through the layers of pain he felt the warmth of her arms and the sweetness of her breath as she whispered, "I was crying over you. I thought...I thought I'd lost you. But you're not dead. Oh," she said, sighing and raining kisses over his mouth, his cheeks, his chin, "you're not dead."

"Not...dead." Not if this pain was any indication. Still, he thought at this moment he'd endure anything, even the fires of hell, just to have her go on holding him, kissing him like this.

"I knew you'd come back to me. I knew it." She couldn't stem the tears. They flowed freely as she pressed salty kisses to his lips.

He let out a shaky laugh, then caught his breath as pain washed over him in great black waves.

"What is it? What...?" She studied the whiteness around his lips, the anguish he couldn't hide.

She released him long enough to mix the contents of the packet with a tumbler of water. Cradling his head, she forced it between his lips. "You must drink this. All of it," she insisted as he tried to push the foul-tasting liquid away. "The doctor said it would ease your pain."

When he drained it, she lowered his head to the pillow and set the glass down.

"One more favor," he managed to whisper.

"Anything. Ask me anything," she said between tears.

"Could you . . . kiss me?"

She framed his face with her hands and brushed her lips over his in the softest, lightest of touches.

"Tell me . . . not dreaming."

"You aren't dreaming, Nevada. I'm real. My kiss is real."

She lifted a hand to wipe away her tears. When she returned her attention to him, she could see that he'd slipped into blessed unconsciousness.

It was pain that woke him. Pain that started in his chest and radiated to every part of his body. Pain that seemed to come in overpowering waves until he was forced to clench his teeth to keep from raging against it.

Had he been in time to save Jade? Or had he finally gambled and lost?

There had been a time in his life when he'd been absolutely fearless. But that had been before Jade. Then he'd had no reason to care. Life before Jade had had no meaning, no purpose. Though she didn't know it, that chance meeting with her had changed him forever.

Who would have thought that she would come back into his life, only to change him once more?

He clenched his teeth against the pain. As it passed, he returned his thoughts to Jade. Seeing another man's hands on her, threatening to soil her, to

hurt her, had caused him absolute terror. He'd been
filled with an unreasonable rage. And he'd rushed in
with no plan, no purpose except to save her. But had
he succeeded?

He thought he remembered seeing her in his
darkest hour. And tasting her kiss. She'd been
weeping, offering comfort. But maybe he'd only
dreamed it. Dreamed those tears, and those soft,
gentle kisses.

That must be it. A dream. Jade Jewel wasn't the
sort who wept. Or freely gave her kisses.

He opened his eyes, and even that small effort cost
him. His lids felt gritty, as though he'd just traveled
across the desert in a dust storm. His tongue was dry
and swollen, his throat parched.

As he adjusted to the dim light, he realized he was
in a bed. A soft feather bed, with satin sheets. Above
his head were lace hangings as delicate as a spider's
web. He breathed in air scented with incense and
perfume.

He turned his head slightly to glance at the fireplace across the room. A log hissed and snapped.
Flames cast dancing shadows on the wall. Above the
huge oak mantel was a jeweled sword beside a gown
of richly colored silk.

Silk. Silk would always remind him of Jade. She
was like that gown of many colors. Shy and sweet.
Bold and obstinate. A woman of so many contra-
dictions.

A slight sound on the other side of the bed had him shifting his gaze. What he saw made all the pain worthwhile.

Jade was curled up on the chaise beside his bed, a blanket draped around her shoulders. Her hair swirled forward to kiss her cheeks. Her bare feet were tucked up beneath her. Her breathing was slow and rhythmic.

He watched the gentle rise and fall of her chest and felt his own heart begin to beat once more. She was safe. It was the only thing that mattered.

As though sensing the change in the figure in the bed, Jade suddenly awoke. As she straightened, the blanket slipped from her shoulders, revealing her blood-soaked gown.

He half rose, a stricken look on his face. "You've...been...hurt." Each word was wrenched from him.

At once she was beside him, her hands touching, soothing, as she studied him with concern. "No. No. I would have been, had it not been for your courage. But you saved me."

"Blood?"

"Yours. I caught you before you could collapse. But your wound was...grave." She shook her head, too overcome for the moment to find the words. At last she whispered, "What you did was the bravest thing I've ever known. You risked your life to save mine."

"Mine wasn't...much of a life."

Tears filled her eyes and she touched a finger to his lips in the sweetest of gestures. "How can you say such a thing? While the rest of us panicked at the sight of Virgil Trent's gun, you calmly faced him down."

"Trent?" He ran his tongue over his lips, struggling to get the words out. "Escape?"

"He's dead."

"Lee Yin?"

"He's fine. The doctor said he'll be as good as new in a few days, thanks to you."

"And you?" Despite the pain, he closed his fingers around her wrist. Her pulse beat was strong and steady and sure.

"I told you. I'm fine. Hush, now. Save your strength. When your wounds have healed, I'll find a way to properly thank you."

He gestured toward the bed. "Whose?"

"Mine. I had you carried up the stairs. This is where you'll stay until your strength returns."

There was so much more he wanted to ask. And things he wanted to say to her. So many things. But it seemed too much effort. Against his will his eyes closed.

As he drifted on a cloud of contentment, he realized he would never need to make another wager on the cards. He'd already gambled for the highest stakes of his life. And won.

Chapter Fourteen

"Lily tells me our patient survived the night." The doctor followed Jade through her sitting room into her bedroom. He paused beside the bed and touched a hand to Nevada's fevered brow. "Is he lucid?"

"He drifts in and out." Jade clasped and unclasped her hands. "He doesn't always make sense."

"That's to be expected. See that he's sponged often to bring the fever down," the doctor said as he examined his patient and changed the dressings. "Fortunately the wound appears clean." He handed her several packets of powder. "Keep him sedated for the next few days. His pain will be severe." He studied her more closely, noting the circles beneath her eyes, and the wrinkled, blood-spattered gown. "Lily also told me that you have appointed yourself his nurse, and that you haven't left his side."

Jade colored slightly. "It was my life he saved."

"I understand," the doctor said more gently. "But your life won't be worth much if you don't take care of your health."

"I will."

He patted her arm. "Good. I'll let myself out, Miss Jewel."

"Thank you, Doctor," she called as he strode away.

"How is he?" Lily paused in the doorway. Behind her was a maid with a linen-covered tray.

The members of the household had determinedly gone about their daily routine, while Jade had remained confined to her rooms, refusing to leave Nevada's side.

Now that darkness had fallen, the sounds drifting up the stairs had become a chorus of voices talking, laughing, occasionally cursing. The high, sweet notes of a violin rose above it all, adding a soothing note.

"He's in much pain, I'm afraid. But he's alive. And for the moment that's all that matters." Jade glanced at the tray. "What's this?"

"Since you won't join us downstairs, I've brought you a meal."

"I'm not hungry."

"Then you will eat to please me," Lily said as she walked past Jade and signaled for the maid to follow. "You refused breakfast and lunch. Since you have decided to be both nurse and servant, you need to keep up your strength." Lily paused to study her young friend. "Did you manage to get any sleep at all?"

"A little." Before Lily could issue a protest she added quickly, "I'll rest later. I promise."

"Drink this." Lily poured tea and thrust a cup into Jade's hand, then uncovered the tray and placed it before her young friend. "Eat," she said imperiously.

Jade did as she was told while perched nervously on the edge of the chair, her gaze never leaving Nevada. It was plain that she was eating simply to appease Lily. She didn't even pause to taste the food.

At a knock on the door she looked up tiredly, but before she could call out, Lily hurried across the room to admit several servants carrying an ornate tub and buckets of steaming water.

"I didn't order a bath," Jade said.

"I did." Ignoring her protests, Lily instructed the maids to pour the water. When that was ready, she took the cup from Jade's hands and said crisply, "You need to refresh yourself."

Jade was too weary to argue. Besides, the sight of steaming water and perfumed soap weakened her resolve. Without a word she stripped and stepped into the tub. A short time later, when her hair had been lathered and rinsed and her body wrapped in warm towels, she sighed in contentment.

"Thank you, Aunt Lily. As usual, you knew better than I. This was exactly what I needed."

"But not all," the older woman said. She held out a silk wrap and nodded approvingly as a maid tied it. "Now you must sleep."

Jade shook her head. "I don't think I could close my eyes. But I'll rest here in the chaise beside the bed."

The older woman seemed prepared to argue, then thought better of it. With a sigh she said, "See that you do." She bent and kissed Jade's cheek, then followed the servants from the room.

As soon as they were gone, Jade moved to the edge of the bed and touched her hand to Nevada's forehead. She sighed in relief. His skin was cool to the touch. The fever had weakened.

For long moments she sat beside him, listening to the silence, broken only by the hiss and snap of the log on the fire.

"Have I died?"

At the sound of Nevada's deep voice, she jumped. "You startled me. I thought you were asleep."

"And I thought I must surely be in heaven."

When she arched a brow he explained, "I saw a vision. The most beautiful woman in the world stepped from a tub, her skin glowing, her dark hair flowing about her like a veil. And she was wearing nothing but the perfect flesh she'd been born with."

Jade couldn't hide her shock. "You saw me?"

A smile tugged at the corners of his lips. "Why, Miss Jewel. Was that you? I thought it was an angel."

She started to push away. "And all this time I believed you to be gravely wounded and fighting for your life."

He caught her hand, stilling her movements. "If I was, an angel's touch saved me and brought me back from the brink."

She allowed herself to relax. "Oh, Nevada, are you truly feeling stronger?"

He caught his breath against the pain. Even the slight movement of his hand had started a fire burning in his chest. "I feel like I've been in a gunfight. And lost."

"You didn't lose. You won. It was your opponent who lost the gunfight."

Funny. He didn't feel like a winner. At the moment the pain was engulfing him in flames. He struggled to hold on to the vision of the beauty he'd seen emerging from the tub. But even that image began to blur and fade.

He paused again, struggling for breath. "As long as you stay with me, I'll know I won."

"I'm staying. I have no intention of leaving your side," she whispered.

"Care to—" he indicated the space beside him "—join me?" When she stiffened, he added, "It's called cuddling."

"Cuddling?"

"Mmm-hmm. And that can lead to all kinds of... interesting things. Of course, in my condition, it will probably only lead to sleep. In which case, you'll manage to get all the rest you need."

Oh, it was tempting. Too tempting. She scurried off the bed and sank onto the lounge, relieved to have put some distance between them.

But as sleep claimed Nevada, Jade listened to his slow, easy breathing and found herself wondering what it would be like to take him up on his offer. To snuggle close beside him. To fall asleep touching him, feeling the steady cadence of each breath.

Annoyed at such thoughts, she pulled the blanket up to her chin. And fell into an exhausted sleep.

For the next week Jade found herself caught up in bursts of frantic activity by day and long, solitary hours at night. Because she refused to leave Nevada's side, all her business had to be conducted in her upper suite of rooms. Through her parlor passed a steady stream of lawyers and prospective buyers for the Golden Dragon. Some saw the elegant building as simply a hotel and restaurant. Others intended to turn it into an exclusive gentleman's club. And one, an Oriental man who had befriended Jade's mother many years before, was willing to pay a fortune to continue operating it as a house of pleasure.

"There is one stipulation, however," he said as he and his lawyer faced Jade across her desk.

A servant poured tea, then discreetly exited the suite.

Jade sipped in silence.

"I want everything to remain as it is," he said. "From the paintings on the walls to the rugs beneath our feet."

Jade arched a brow. "The furnishings are worth a great deal. Some were brought from China. Others from Europe. I could never replace them."

"I know their value. And I am willing to pay a fair price. But they are a necessary part of my plan to continue the tradition established by your honorable mother, Ahn Lin. Without them, the customers will seek their pleasures elsewhere."

Jade swallowed. She had intended to take much of this with her, to soften the harshness of her new Texas venture. But this was a chance to simplify. She wouldn't have to deal with the confusion of inventory lists and shipping, not to mention the items that would be damaged en route.

"I suppose we can come to some sort of arrangement." She nodded toward a framed portrait on the wall, showing her mother as a young girl in China. "There are some items I cannot part with."

His smile broadened. "Of course. If you will draw up an inventory, my lawyer and I will exclude those items of a personal nature."

She studied the document that he presented her. It offered more money than she'd ever hoped for. How could she refuse? But still she demurred.

"I will consider your offer, Chang Lu. But the women who work here are not part of the deal."

His dark brows drew together in a frown. "Yours
are the finest women in San Francisco. My patrons
will demand the best. Why can they not remain with
me?"

"The decision must be theirs," she said firmly.
"They must be free to stay or go." And she desperately hoped they would choose to go with her. To a
new beginning in Texas.

As his wounds slowly healed and his strength returned, Nevada saw Jade in a new light. Always before, he had assumed she led a pampered life of ease,
surrounded by wealth and luxury. Now he regarded
her also as a businesswoman, who worked hard to
maintain a high standard of living, not only for herself but for all who were employed at the Golden
Dragon.

Through the closed door of the bedroom he overheard everything. The business meetings. The occasional reprimand when one of the employees
disobeyed a rule of the house. And Lily's carefully
chosen words of advice, usually delivered in a voice
devoid of emotion.

He saw, too, the long hours, when the others were
asleep, that Jade spent going over the expenses,
checking invoices, recording everything in her ledgers.

Despite her sheltered upbringing, she had an
amazing well of knowledge and an excellent business sense. But in one area of her life she was woe-

fully lacking. Though she directed an army of women trained to please men, she had never joined their ranks.

A smile touched Nevada's lips as he listened to the sound of her musical voice in the next room. As soon as his strength returned, he vowed, he would be the one to teach her.

Besides the potential buyers to deal with, there were the women looking for work. Some of them were recent immigrants desperate to survive. A few were girls from the street, hoping for something better. Because there were so many of them in San Francisco, Jade could afford to choose only the best. But even with Lily's help, she found the interviews distasteful. The tales told by many of the young women brought tears to her eyes. Tales of beatings, of brutality by men who claimed to love them.

After one especially unpleasant interview, Jade entered her bedroom and sank onto the chaise.

"You should be here," Nevada said gruffly, patting the bed, "where you can get your proper rest."

At the sound of his voice she sat up. "You're awake. Do you need anything?"

He shook his head. "Nothing."

"I could have a servant bring you a tray."

"Later. Right now I don't want you to move. You've been through enough for one day."

She glanced at him, amazed that he should be concerned for her when he was the one who had suffered so greatly. "What are you talking about?"

"I overheard the interview with the young French girl. She painted a pretty grim picture."

Jade gripped her hands together and looked away. "I should be used to it by now. It is always the same. Abuse at the hands of cruel fathers or husbands. No safe place to sleep. A woman alone, afraid, desperate. None of the stories are new. But each time, I find myself getting angry. It isn't fair. Everyone should have a mother and father to love and protect them."

For the space of several moments he was quiet. Then he muttered, "Nobody ever said life was fair, Jade. For every girl like you, who had loving parents, there is one like the girl who just left here."

"What about you, Nevada?" she asked suddenly. "Were your parents kind and loving?"

Before he could reply there was a knock on the door and a servant entered, carrying a tray. Jade directed her to set it on the nightstand beside the bed.

It took the efforts of both women to help Nevada to a sitting position, with mounds of pillows supporting him. When the maid took her leave, Jade picked up a fork and began to feed him.

"You'd better be careful," he muttered between bites. "I may learn to like this kind of treatment."

She avoided meeting his gaze, and busied herself with his food. But when she looked up, she felt the jolt of those clear amber eyes all the way to her toes.

To cover her confusion she commanded, "Open your mouth."

He did as he was told, and accepted the food from her hand. As her fingers touched his lips, Jade realized it was the most purely sensual feeling she had ever known. The act of feeding him was such an intimate gesture, she found herself trembling.

She tried to turn away, to hide the color that stained her cheeks. He caught her chin. As his gaze burned over her, she felt a rush of heat that left her weak.

He brought his other hand to her shoulder and drew her fractionally closer, all the while staring into her eyes. "One day soon my strength will return." His voice was low and deep and rough with anger as his thumb traced her lips. "On that day I'm going to see that you stop pushing yourself so hard. I'll be strong enough for both of us, so that you can get the rest you need."

His touch was as shocking as a kiss. With her hand against his chest she resisted being drawn into the web of his charm. "I'll never let anyone else be strong for me. I was taught to depend on myself, Nevada."

He pulled her close and kissed her, hard and quick. It was as shocking as a jolt of lightning, and both of them reacted as though they'd been struck.

Jade pulled back until his hand at her shoulder stopped her. But even that simple movement had taken its toll, and Nevada was forced to lie back against the pillows.

"You see. Your strength has not yet returned," she said as firmly as she could manage. "You know the rules. You need to eat if you're ever going to leave that bed."

"Soon, Jade. Very soon," he muttered. "And then we're going to toss out all the rules. And write new ones."

She could feel his heartbeat strong and steady against her palm. Her own was racing like a runaway stage.

He felt it, too. And experienced a sense of satisfaction that he could have such an effect on her. It would seem that the cool proprietor of the Golden Dragon was feeling more than a little flustered.

He intended to cause her a great deal more discomfort before he was through. Oh, yes. A great deal more discomfort, he promised himself. He'd test her strength to the limit. And his own.

Chapter Fifteen

Jade discovered that, as the days passed and Nevada began to mend, sleep was increasingly difficult. To her horror, much of her night was spent thinking about the man enjoying the comfort of her bed. And what it would feel like to join him there.

Such thoughts ran counter to everything she had been taught. She could hear her old tutor's voice as she'd instructed, "Remember, child, that lust is like opium. It weakens, even while giving the illusion of strength. In order to be strong, a woman must not need the things a man offers. Instead, the woman must make the man desire what only she can give. Then she will be in a position of power, of strength."

Why, Jade wondered, must everything come down to power and strength? But when she'd asked her tutor, the old woman's reply had always been, "If you had ever endured bondage, you would not question. You would know that the weak are always dominated by the strong. It is enough to know that you must never show your enemy your weakness. Instead, show only strength.''

"Are men our enemies?" Jade had asked.

"I look upon them," the old teacher had said with a smile, "as necessary evils."

With such words ringing in her mind, Jade again studied the sleeping figure of Nevada. It was true that a man had tried to hurt her. But it was also true that another had risked his own life to save hers. Surely that was not the sign of one who would dominate.

Oh, if only her honorable father was alive. She knew he would have had answers to all her questions. And would have helped her chart a course through this maze.

She turned away, fighting a wave of confusion and frustration.

Jade climbed the stairs, her mind reeling from the documents she had just signed. As she stepped into her bedroom she stopped in midstride. Nevada was standing by a basin of water. All he wore was a towel.

"What are you doing out of bed?"

He turned. "I never thought I'd say this, but I'm tired of being pampered. I'm sick of feather beds and satin sheets. And being spoon-fed by an angel."

"But the doctor said you needed more time to heal." She started across the room, then skidded to a halt.

It was one thing to see him weak and wounded, fighting for his life. But now, standing here half-naked, he exuded strength and masculine virility.

The towel rode low on his hips. His feet were bare, as was his chest. Little drops of water still clung to his hair and lashes.

He shot her a dangerous smile. "I think I might have taken on too much. Would you mind helping me back to bed?"

She stepped beside him and he draped an arm around her shoulder. Up close he smelled of lavender soap. It was such a contrast to his rugged looks, it made her smile. The feel of his bare arm and chest was deliciously wicked, causing her breath to back up in her throat.

Leaning heavily on her, he moved slowly across the room until they reached the bed.

"Can you make it?" she asked.

He brought his lips close to her ear. "You might have to ease me down a bit."

She couldn't hide her trembling response. That only made him bolder. "I'm losing my balance. You'd better hold on to me."

Alarmed, she caught him around the waist just as he tumbled backward. He landed on the bed, pulling her down on top of him.

He moaned slightly and she struggled to free herself. "Oh, dear, I've hurt you."

"Mmm." His arms came around her, pinning her to the length of him. Her lips hovered a fraction above his. "But it's a good hurt."

"A good . . . ?" She lifted her head and shot him a look of disbelief.

But in that same instant he tangled both hands in her hair and forced her head down until her lips were brushing his.

"I think you should kiss away the hurt." The teasing laughter in his eyes faded, to be replaced with a look that had her heart almost stopping.

"No. We . . . mustn't."

"You don't want to kiss me?"

She tasted his breath, warm and tempting. The mere brush of his lips had started her blood pulsing, her heartbeat racing out of control.

"No."

"Liar."

"I'm not—"

His kiss swallowed her protest.

The last time he'd kissed her, he'd convinced himself that it was all a dream. And that the heat flowing like lava through his veins was a result of the fever. But this time there was no doubt. The kiss was real. The woman in his arms was real. And the heat flowing between them was the result of emotions too strong to contain.

He took her mouth, devoured it like a starving man. But it wasn't enough. In a frenzy of need he rolled to his side, taking her with him. He wanted her, needed her. All of her.

She sighed as he lingered over her lips, as though he'd just discovered them and couldn't get enough. But as she began to relax, he took the kiss deeper.

The silk of her gown was roughly torn aside. His mouth plundered her throat, her neck, her shoulder. But nothing would satisfy his hunger. It was consuming him. Consuming them both.

After her first moment of stunned surprise, she found herself caught up in a passion that ran roughshod over the rules. This was not as her tutor had described a carefully planned seduction or an erotic night of pleasure. This was passion. Need. Harddriving need that had somehow caught them up, then slipped out of control. The moment his lips began to weave their magic, she was lost.

He feasted on her lips. The more he took, the more she gave. But neither of them could get enough. There was a fever in their blood, driving them mad with heat. They dove into the kiss again and again, but nothing would satisfy the hunger.

Nevada knew he was taking her too far, too fast.

Struggling for breath, he lifted his head and caught her by the shoulders. Her eyes were wide, her lips swollen from his kisses. Her breathing was as ragged as his.

"I guess I'm not as strong as I thought." He kissed the tip of her nose, then fell back against the pillows.

She tried to speak, but it took too much effort. Her pulse was still pounding, her chest heaving. At last she managed to whisper, "Why do you say that?"

"Don't you know how beautiful you are, Jade? How tempted I am every time I look at you? If I was completely healed, we wouldn't be talking right now." He pressed the back of his hand over his closed eyes. "We'd be finishing what we started."

She watched him struggle for control. Very carefully she slid from the bed and gathered the remnants of her torn bodice in her hand. She didn't mind the torn silk. What she did mind was the flood of feelings she couldn't seem to still.

He thought she was beautiful. And he wanted her. Was tempted by her. Her heart felt so light, she feared it would fly away.

When she turned back to study him, he had rolled to his side. His breathing was slow and steady, his eyes tightly closed, as if he were dead to the world.

But she felt more alive than at any time in her life.

"I see you managed to sleep," Lily said as she swept into the room.

"Like an infant."

"And Nevada?"

Jade touched a finger to her lips and led the way to the other room. "His fever has completely disappeared and his wound is healing. But he is still in much pain. He does not speak of it, but I see it in his eyes.''

A servant drew open the draperies before tossing a fresh log on the embers.

Within minutes another maid entered bearing a linen-covered tray. Jade ignored her food while she tossed the last of the soiled bandages onto the fire.

''We have servants for such things,'' Lily said dryly.

''This is something I must see to myself.''

''I realize in the beginning you were grateful, but now that Nevada is healing, I think it is time you stepped back and allowed the maids to see to him,'' Lily said firmly.

She had seen what was developing between the gambler and her young friend. And it alarmed her more than she cared to admit.

''It isn't just gratitude.'' Jade stood, smoothing her damp palms down her skirt, searching for the words. ''We are linked now, he and I. It is because of him that I am alive. For I truly believe Virgil Trent would have killed me after he'd tired of... of the other things he had in mind.'' She met Lily's glance. ''So you see, Aunt Lily, it is much more than gratitude. I realize now that my life is forever joined to his, in the ancient ways of my mother's people.''

Lily's mouth was a tight line of disapproval as she spread honey on a biscuit and handed it to her young friend. Jade refused, unable to think about eating.

"You are tired and emotional," Lily said with as much control as she could manage. "It is to be expected that you would be confused after all that has happened. In the short time since you have returned home, you have been attacked, you have had to deal with a seriously wounded man and you have had the responsibility of selling your mother's family business. No wonder you are so emotional."

Jade gave her friend a quick smile. "I do not speak merely from emotion. I've had a great many hours to think this through, Aunt Lily."

"And what have you been thinking about?"

"I think it is time I learned firsthand what goes on behind closed doors in a house of pleasure."

The older woman found a chair and sank into it. Though she struggled to keep her tone light, she couldn't hide the slight edge to her voice. "And Nevada is to be your teacher?"

Jade's smile grew. "Can you think of a better one?"

Beneath the show of bravado, Lily thought she detected a hint of nerves. It was all she needed to drive home her point. "What we offer is a service. What you are considering is something far different."

"What do you mean?"

"What you are thinking comes from your heart. And hearts are very delicate, Jade. They can be broken. Furthermore, as the proprietor of the Golden

Dragon, it is not in your best interests to lower yourself to that of a common employee.''

"But I want to learn about love, Aunt Lily. And who better to teach me than the man who nearly gave his life for me?"

"One cannot learn about love, Jade. There are no schools for such things. And no tutors.''

"Then how do people learn it? And survive it?''

"Some manage very well. Others merely muddle through, or fail miserably. Look at your father and mother.'' Her tone softened. "I have never seen two people more deeply in love. But despite what they felt, they never managed to live together. Except for a few joyous nights, they led completely separate lives. Even their mutual love for you could not keep them together.'' She got to her feet and crossed to her young friend. "Are you willing to settle for what your parents had?''

Jade tried to dismiss the thread of fear that had suddenly slipped through her protective armor. "I don't know. I only know that I feel things for Nevada that I never felt for anyone else. And I want him to feel the same way about me.''

"What we want in this life and what we get are often very different. You must decide if you will give your heart or merely your body to this man.''

"Why can't I do both?''

Lily gave her a sad little smile. "Some do. They call it love and marriage. But it is not for women like us.''

Women like us.

The words stung.

"What we do in the Golden Dragon must never be confused with love, Jade. What I see before me is a very confused, very dishonest young woman."

"Dishonest!" Jade was horrified at her friend's use of such a word. Of all the things in her life, she was proudest of the fact that she had always been honest—about herself, her past, her future dreams.

"You alone know what is in your heart, Jade," Lily said more gently. "You alone can judge the honesty or dishonesty of your motives. Now I will leave you to search your heart for the answers. And I pray you make the right decisions. For they will affect the rest of your life."

When the door closed behind her, Jade began to pace while Lily's words continued to play through her mind. Could she give herself to Nevada and still have control of her heart? Or was she playing a dangerous game that might prove to be her undoing?

Suddenly she stopped her pacing and went very still. It didn't matter. The truth was, nothing mattered except Nevada. She wanted him. Not out of gratitude. Nor out of a sense of duty for what he'd done. She simply wanted him. Wanted to lie with him in the big feather bed and feel his strong arms around her, while his kisses made her blood run hot. She wanted him to teach her the ways of men and women. Not the textbook lessons she'd learned from her tutor, not the deliciously wicked things the girls in the house often confided to her about pleasing men. She wanted him to lead her to that magical, wonderful height of passion that made two perfectly sensible people like her father and mother forsake everything but each other.

Suddenly overcome with anticipation, she ran from the room and went in search of Lily. Despite her friend's misgivings, Jade knew Lily could be counted on to help her prepare for the most important night of her life.

Nevada lay very still. If he hadn't heard it himself, he wouldn't believe it.

Jade was his for the taking.

Since the first time he'd seen her, he'd dreamed of a hundred ways to seduce her. She was all he wanted. All he'd ever hoped for. The mere thought of her, warm and willing, coming to his bed like a bride, had him fully aroused.

And yet, despite the excitement, he couldn't seem to put aside Lily's warning. Was it love Jade was feeling? Or mere gratitude? His hand tightened at his side. Any gunman with a quick draw and a steady aim could have done what he had. As for her curiosity about men and women, he realized that he might have played some small part in her sexual awakening. But it was to be expected at her age. If he hadn't come along, some other cowboy would have been happy to be her teacher.

But was it love?

He knew what was in his own heart. From the first moment he'd seen her, he'd wanted her. And somehow, without his choosing, it had become love. Whenever he was with her, he found himself thinking about love and marriage and forever after.

Forever after. The stuff of dreams. And in his case, foolish ones. He was all wrong for a woman like Jade Jewel. If she knew the truth about him, she would close her heart to him forever. Not very comforting, but the truth had to be faced. Before he did something they'd both regret.

He slipped out of bed and strode to the window, peering down at the activity in the street below. Jade wasn't the only one who'd been doing some heavy thinking. All this time on his hands had helped him clear his mind. It was time to face some tough facts.

He'd come to San Francisco to see if his old life still fit. The truth was, it didn't. He'd finally had his fill of this town and the life of a gambler and drifter.

The niche he'd carved for himself in Hanging Tree might have been based on a lie, but it had been a satisfying one. The problem was, once the citizens of that town knew the truth, they would have no use for him. Still, he owed them that much. Regardless of the outcome, he had to go back and face them. And reveal all his dark secrets.

He walked stiffly across the room to retrieve his shirt and boots. By the time he'd managed to dress and pull on his gun belt, his forehead and upper lip were beaded with sweat from the effort.

He hated this weakness. But he knew his strength would return if he was patient. He wouldn't be able to travel more than a few miles a day. But at least he'd put temptation behind him. And maybe one night, if he lived long enough, he'd be able to close his eyes without seeing Jade's beautiful face in his dreams.

Until then he'd consider it the price he had to pay to make up for a past riddled with shame.

Chapter Sixteen

"Oh, Lily. Be happy for me."

With a quick hug, Jade spun away. Her green satin slippers hardly made a sound on the carpeted floor as she danced along the hallway toward her suite. When she reached the door she paused and smoothed her damp palms down her skirt.

After voicing her initial protest, Lily had listened to her young friend's arguments in silence. Then, realizing she could not change Jade's mind, she had behaved exactly as Jade had hoped. She had taken charge, not only of Jade's physical appearance but of her mental state, as well—calming, soothing, coaching.

An army of servants had been summoned to prepare a bath. Afterward, Jade's hair and skin were perfumed. Dressed in her finest green silk gown, the young woman had wriggled impatiently as a maid arranged her hair in a smooth coil of black silk, pulled to one side to cascade over her breast.

"What will I say?" She lifted imploring eyes to her old friend.

"Words are not necessary. When Nevada sees you, he will know."

"I don't understand."

"Oh, Jade." Lily turned the young woman toward the looking glass. "Look at your eyes. The love you are feeling is there for him to read." She caught her friend's hand and placed it over her heart. "Feel how your pulse races. Like you have been running up Nob Hill. It adds color to your cheeks and puts a sparkle in your eyes. You need not say a word. Nevada will know."

Jade had studied her reflection, but could see none of the changes Lily described. No matter. She didn't want to look at herself. She wanted to look at Nevada.

Now, at the door to her suite, anticipating all the pleasures that awaited her on the other side, she touched a hand to her necklace and whispered a prayer.

"Honorable Father, I know you understand all the fear and confusion, and the anticipation and love that is in my heart at this moment. Please give me your blessing on what I am about to do."

She stepped into the room, then paused in consternation.

Except for the light of the fire, the room was in darkness. There were no lanterns lit. No candles gleamed in sconces along the wall.

As her eyes adjusted to the dim light, she could see that the bed was empty. Her heart seemed to stop.

"I've been waiting for you."

At the sound of Nevada's voice, she spun around. He was seated in a chair in the corner. The tip of his cigar glowed red in the darkness.

She swallowed, then found her voice. "When I saw the empty bed I was . . . I was afraid you'd left."

"I thought about it. But I couldn't leave without seeing you."

Her smile returned. "That's good." Then she remembered Lily's advice. *Approach him slowly, seductively, like a tigress. Let your body say all the things your mind is thinking.*

Jade moved toward him, her hips unconsciously swaying in the way of a woman who knows she is beautiful. She noted that his hand holding the cigar halted in midair. A good sign. She slowed her walk even more.

He was mesmerized. With each step his throat closed until it was impossible to breathe. She was a vision in green silk. Her gown molded to her body like a second skin. And hers was a body like no other. Slim and lithe and perfect.

"I'm glad to see you out of bed. That must mean you're feeling stronger."

He tossed the cigar into the fire and got to his feet. "Not nearly strong enough." Especially now that she was here with him, looking like something out of a dream.

Her smile was radiant. "I have a surprise for you, Nevada."

As she drew close, he breathed in the exotic fragrance of Oriental flowers and spices. It was like no other perfume he'd ever known.

"Before you tell me your surprise, I think I'd better share my news."

She paused, blinked. This wasn't part of her plan. "News?"

He'd had hours to think this through, but the look of confusion on her lovely face was like a knife to his heart. If he wasn't so convinced that it was for her own good, he'd back down right now and take the pleasure she was offering. Instead he plunged ahead. "I'm leaving San Francisco."

"Leaving! When?"

"Now. Tonight." He saw her sway, as though struck, and forced himself to continue. "I was just waiting for you to return so I could tell you goodbye."

"Goodbye..." She caught hold of the back of the chair for support. "Where are you going?"

"There's a job waiting for me. In Nevada."

"Nevada." She was babbling like a parrot, but she couldn't seem to stop herself. The pain was so blinding she couldn't see through the blur of tears. "That's where you got your name, isn't it?"

"About that name." Her smile was gone. The smile that had been brighter than a hundred candles. In its place was a trembling in her lips that she couldn't hide. With every word he hated himself. Hated what he was doing to her. But it had to be done. Quickly. Cleanly. Like the bite of a razor-sharp hunting knife. And he knew all about knives. And guns. And cruelty. "The name Nevada was a lie. I made it up. Like everything else in my life."

"Everything?" Her head came up, reminding him of a wounded deer. "Was everything you said to me a lie, as well?"

He reached a hand to touch her, then seemed to think better of it and took a step back out of reach. His voice was thick. "No, Jade. That may have been the only truth I've ever spoken. You're very special."

"So special that you have to leave me." There were no tears now. Her eyes were hard, glittering chips of onyx, and her voice had gone flat. "At least tell me your real name before you go."

It was tempting. She was tempting. What he wanted was to pull her into his arms and beg her to forget everything he'd just said. To take what she was offering and lose himself in her. Instead he turned away and crossed the room.

As he walked he said, "You don't want to know my name. It's better if you just think of me as Nevada."

At the door he paused, but refused to turn around. He couldn't afford to look at her. Not if he wanted to make it out of here.

With all the willpower he could summon he said, "I'll never forget you, Jade. I wish you only good things for the rest of your life."

She felt him pulling away from her slowly, like the dressings on his wounds that she had so carefully cleansed. Only now he was healed. Strong. Free. And she was the wound. Raw. Bleeding. Numb.

And then he was gone.

Long afterward she could still hear the sound of his footsteps retreating. Leaving her alone with the silence. The horrible, unbearable silence.

"Has she eaten?" Lily met the servant in the hallway outside Jade's room.

The maid shook her head and lifted a napkin to display the contents of the tray. "Not even a drop of tea."

"Four days, and still she grieves." Lily squared her shoulders and strode into Jade's suite.

The parlor was empty. In the bedroom the air was heavy with incense. Jade was standing before a hastily arranged altar, head bowed, hands folded.

"Jade."

At the sound of Lily's voice, Jade's head came up sharply.

"I must speak with you, my friend."

When the young woman turned, Lily was surprised to note that, despite her obvious weight loss, she appeared calm and composed.

"And I must speak with you, Aunt Lily. I have been conversing with my honorable parents. They have advised me to get on with my life."

"Excellent advice." Lily peered at her. "Will you be able to do it?"

Jade took a deep breath, and actually gave a wan smile. "You told me that the heart is a delicate thing. You were wrong. I know now that a heart can be shattered beyond repair and still continue to beat." She led the way to the parlor and sat down behind her desk. "Chang Lu sent word that he wishes to take possession of the Golden Dragon at once." She spread out an assortment of documents and picked up a pen, dipping it in a pot of ink. "I will arrange to have my personal possessions shipped ahead. And I will charter several coaches to take us to our new business in Hanging Tree."

Lily folded her hands in her lap. "I'm relieved that you have ... sufficiently recovered to take charge of your life once more. Now I can only hope that you are strong enough to hear what I must tell you."

Jade's hand holding the pen paused in midair.

Lily looked away, avoiding her young friend's eyes. "As you may have noticed, Senator Hammond has been a ... very close friend of mine for several years."

Jade waited in silence, her brow arched in question.

"The senator has asked me to remain here in San Francisco, so that we can continue our... relationship."

Jade lowered her hand, the pen forgotten. "What would you do here in San Francisco? Remain in the employ of Chang Lu?"

"No. The senator wants to set me up in a lovely home on Nob Hill. I will have servants, and a driver for my carriage, and a life of ease."

"But the senator is married," Jade said softly.

Lily lifted her head to meet her friend's troubled eyes. "I am well aware of that fact. He and I can never be more than... friends. But it is enough for me. He cares for me. And respects me. And that is more than a woman like me could ever hope for."

A woman like me. The words tore at Jade's already wounded heart.

The two gazed at each other. Jade's eyes filled with tears at the thought of losing her oldest, dearest friend.

Lily's eyes also filled as she asked, "Can you forgive me for deserting you?"

"Hush now." Slowly Jade got to her feet and came around the desk. When she opened her arms, Lily fell into her embrace.

"I am truly sorry, Jade. I had so wanted to ease your burden, not add to it."

Jade touched her friend's cheek. "Burden? Never. You have been my friend, my teacher, my fierce protector. I desire only your happiness." Almost shyly she asked, "You are certain that you are happy with this arrangement?"

"Very happy. I care very much for Senator Hammond."

"I would ask you one favor."

Lily brushed away her tears. "Anything."

"If something should happen between the two of you—if you should ever find yourself friendless in this town, promise me that you will come to me in Hanging Tree. For my home is always open to you."

"Oh, Jade." The older woman burst into fresh tears. "You deserve so much more. Friends who will never desert you. A man to love you, and cherish you, and marry you. A chance to be part of a family. A real family."

"You and the other women here at the Golden Dragon are all the family I need," she whispered against her friend's cheek.

She felt Lily stiffen, then push away. "There is more. And it is equally painful. But I can't bear to burden you further."

Jade waited, her eyes troubled. "Tell me."

"The women who work here are afraid to leave. Texas is so vast, so...primitive. They have heard so many frightening stories about it." She took a deep breath and said, "They have agreed to stay on and work for Chang Lu."

She expected Jade to weep. Or at least to struggle beneath the weight of this added blow. Instead, Jade pinned her with an incredulous look. "How many of the women?"

"All of them."

"How do you know?"

"They have been talking among themselves. They love you, Jade. But they are truly afraid of change."

"I see." Jade turned and walked to her desk. For long minutes she stared at the ledgers. Then she lifted her head and said, "Thank you, Lily. Leave me now. I have much work to do."

"I could help...."

Jade shook her head. "I must do this alone."

Alone. Alone. The word seemed to echo in her mind.

When she heard the door close, she continued to stare at the papers littering her desk. Then, taking a deep breath, she picked up the pen and dipped it once more into the pot of ink. There were documents to sign. Ledgers to tally. Personal items to be packed. And the final page to be written in the life she had always known here in San Francisco.

Having sent her trunks ahead, Jade packed her remaining belongings in a tapestry bag and handed it to a servant.

Alone in her room, she walked to the window for a final glimpse of the city of her birth. San Francisco was so lovely it took her breath away. She loved the view of the docks, with the ships from all over the world. She loved the crowded streets, the ebb and flow of humanity, the mansions of Nob Hill, the hovels of the newly arrived immigrants.

She turned away and cast a last look at the luxurious suite of rooms. Then she made her way down the stairs, pausing to study the gleaming chandeliers, the ornate rugs, the familiar pictures on the walls.

Home, her heart whispered. And yet, not home. She felt torn between the opulence of the place she was leaving and the simplicity that awaited her at the end of her journey.

If her mother and father had still been alive, there would have been no choice. This place suited her as nothing else ever would. But without them it was just a beautiful, empty shell.

Besides, though it still seemed strange to admit it, her heart now lay in the dusty little town of Hanging Tree, Texas. Not because of Nevada, or Reverend Wade Weston, or whatever he chose to call himself now, she told herself sternly. But because of three strangers who had become her family. Perhaps, she realized, they were the only true friends she would ever have. She shared something unshakable with Diamond, Pearl and Ruby. The blood of her honorable father ran through each of them. They were a family now. Her only true family.

With dry eyes she embraced Lily and the other women, offering each of them a word of thanks, or a wish for future happiness.

Then she was helped aboard the stage. Without a backward glance she set off on her journey home.

Home, her heart whispered. She was not leaving it. She was returning to it.

Chapter Seventeen

Jade stifled a yawn. This last leg of the journey would be the longest. And the loneliest. The rest of the passengers had departed at the Spanish mission at Standing Rock. She was the only one bound for Hanging Tree. In two days she would be home.

She stared out the window at the passing landscape. The barren stretch of desert, punctuated by towering buttes and mounds of rocks that defied gravity, oddly stirred her senses.

Who would have believed she could learn to love this wilderness? But each mile that brought her closer to the Jewel ranch brought a lightness to her heart.

She settled back and closed her eyes. Minutes later the sound of thundering hoofbeats had her sitting up straight. Peering out the window, she caught sight of four horsemen riding at breakneck speed toward the stage. From the other window she could see more horsemen coming toward them. Six in all, firing rifles and shouting for the driver to halt.

For a few terrifying minutes the driver actually tried to outrun the band of outlaws. The stage swayed from side to side, tossing Jade around like a rag doll. But when a gunshot tore through the driver's shoulder he struggled to rein in the team. At last they came to a shuddering stop.

Jade, who had been thrown to the floor of the stage, pulled herself to a sitting position and peered nervously from the window. The gunmen, wearing bandannas over their faces, had surrounded the stage and were ordering the driver down.

Someone yanked open the door. Jade shrank back as a man shouted, "Well, look what I found." He grasped her by the arm and dragged her from the coach.

The leader, who was still astride his horse, couldn't hide his surprise. Or his jubilation. At the sight of her his hand went to his shoulder, which still bore the pain of her knife. "Well, well. So we meet again."

Before she could reach a hand to the knife at her waist he called, "Tie her. And see that she's searched. She's not going to get a second chance to attack me."

"With pleasure." One of the men viciously twisted her arms behind her back and bound her wrists, while another yanked the knife from her sash and tossed it to the leader. That done, he ran his hands up her skirts and across her breasts, all the while sneering each time she flinched.

"Is this your only passenger?" the leader asked the driver as he tucked Jade's knife into his waistband.

"Yes." The old man clutched his wound, trying vainly to stem the flow of blood. "But you should be warned. This is Miss Jade Jewel, owner of one of the biggest ranches in Texas. Her wranglers won't take kindly to her being mistreated."

"Is that so?" The leader studied her a minute, then calmly stretched out his arm and pointed it at the driver. The movement engaged a small pistol hidden in his sleeve.

At the explosion of sound, Jade let out a scream and was forced to watch in horror as the driver dropped to his knees. Blood spilled from his chest, forming a mottled pool in the sand. He moaned and writhed, driven half-mad with the pain, but no one went to his aid.

"Damned little bullets," one of the men said. "How long do you think it'll take him to die, Ned?"

"Don't know. But we don't have time to wait." The leader stretched out his arm a second time and fired.

The driver gasped, then went limp as the pool of blood around him made ever-widening circles.

Jade went rigid with shock. Before she could recover her senses, the leader shouted, "Unhitch those horses. And bring the woman with us. She's going to pay for what she did to me. And when I'm finished with her, the rest of you can have what's left of her."

With her hands still tied she was lifted into a saddle, and her horse's reins passed to one of the men. Without a backward glance at the man they had shot, the band of outlaws took off at a gallop.

Jade felt a wave of hysteria rising up, threatening to choke her. She was in the clutches of crazed gunmen. And they would leave no witnesses alive to testify to their madness.

Nevada reined in his mount at the top of a ridge. He stared in surprise at the abandoned stage, then spotted a body in the grass. With a muttered oath he nudged his horse into a run.

He knew even before he touched a hand to the man's throat that he was dead. But from the freshness of the blood, he surmised it had been a recent kill.

He turned away and examined the horses' tracks that surrounded the stage. One bore a distinctive half-moon indentation. Nevada's eyes narrowed in recognition. Ned Garland. No one knew better than he that Garland had absolutely no conscience. In fact, he'd probably thoroughly enjoyed killing the helpless stage driver.

As soon as he returned to Hanging Tree, he'd have to report this to the marshal.

Nevada had started to pull himself into the saddle when he spotted a tapestry valise, half-hidden under the passenger seat. The bumpy ride had apparently tossed it around. He pulled it from its hiding place and opened it. His heart nearly stopped.

It contained a few simple articles. Fragrant soap. A brush and comb. A shawl. And at the very bottom a gown of green silk, with a mandarin collar and frog fasteners.

With a heart-wrenching moan he lifted the gown to his face and breathed in the fragrance of exotic spices and flowers.

Jade. God in heaven, Jade was at the mercy of Ned Garland.

Nevada clutched the valise to his heart like a talisman as he began to follow the trail of the horsemen.

They had been in the saddle for hours. Though the gunmen seemed to know where they were headed, Jade had lost all sense of direction. They followed a twisting route over roaring rivers, across dry gulches, along narrow, rocky ridges. Their band stopped several times, pausing beside streams to drink and fill their canteens, but they never once offered water to their captive.

As the sun sank lower in the west, Jade's spirits sank with it. For she knew that as soon as darkness covered the land they would have to stop for the night. And then, for her, the real terror would begin.

The sod hut was built into the side of a hill. For a person unaware it was there, it would have been impossible to see. It was the perfect hideout for a band of outlaws. Without any moonlight to guide them, the gunmen moved unerringly toward it.

They left their horses in a nearby wood, where they wouldn't be spotted by passing riders.

"Bring the woman," the leader called as he dismounted and strode toward the hut.

One of the men dragged Jade from her horse and hauled her roughly along.

"I'm hungry," someone said. "Think the woman can cook?"

"I didn't bring her here to cook," the leader growled. "If you want to eat, fix it yourself. As for me, I'm going to finish this whiskey. Then me and the woman are going to have some fun."

Jade's hands had long ago gone numb. Now, as she was shoved toward a corner of the filthy hut, she stumbled and fell. No one helped her. Instead, they laughed as she struggled to sit.

She huddled with her back against the wall. She was cold and hungry and weary beyond belief. And a feeling of terror threatened to paralyze her. But she knew that unless she stayed alert and awake, she would be lost.

If there was even a single chance of escaping this hell, she was determined to risk it.

The outlaws were sprawled on the floor in a semi-circle around the fireplace. They had been passing the jug back and forth for over an hour. With each tick of the clock their crude remarks and coarse laughter grew.

The leader drunkenly swiveled his head and fixed Jade with a look of pure hatred.

"Come here, woman."

When she didn't move, he shuffled to his feet and crossed the room to stand over her. He lowered his voice. "When I give you an order, I expect it to be followed. Now get up."

With a look of defiance she remained on the floor.

Muttering a string of oaths, he reached down and hauled her to her feet. "Looks like I'm going to have to teach you some manners," he said with an air of triumph.

He turned to one of his men. "Hand me that torch."

The man retrieved a long stick. One end had been wrapped with cloth and tar. He plunged it into the flames. When it caught fire he handed it to the leader, who brought it so close to Jade's face she flinched. "You saw what I did to that stage driver. His was an easy death next to the one I have planned for you, unless you do as you're told. Understand?"

She swallowed but refused to acknowledge him.

His hand fisted in her hair and he pulled her head back until tears sprang to her eyes. His other hand held the flaming torch inches from her face. But still she refused to give voice to her fear.

"Looks like she needs a few more lessons, Ned," one of the men called.

The others threw back their heads and roared.

"And I'm just the one to give 'em to her. First lesson," he began, bringing the flame perilously close to her hair.

Just then the door to the hut was kicked in and a volley of gunfire had the men diving for cover. A couple of the men looked as if they'd seen a ghost. Several others went for their guns, but more gunfire had them dropping their weapons and scrambling to take cover.

It was a scene of complete confusion, with guns roaring like thunder and bodies writhing and twisting in pain. Despite the fact that a lone gunman was facing half a dozen opponents, he never backed down or took cover. He merely fired until there was no one left to return his fire.

As suddenly as it had started, it ended. A deadly silence settled over the tiny hut as Ned dragged Jade from behind an overturned bench where they had taken cover.

Jade heard Nevada's voice. "Better let her go, Ned, or I'll have to blow you away, too. And you know I'm just the one who can."

Though she had seen him face down gunmen before, she had never heard such raw fury in his tone, or seen such rage contorting his face into a mask. It was a face, a voice she didn't recognize.

The leader stared around at the carnage, then faced the man in the doorway. There was a look of astonishment in his eyes. "Danny. What the hell...?"

"I told you to keep looking over your shoulder, Ned, because one day I'd come back."

"Okay," Ned said. "You had your revenge. But if you think you're going to shoot me, too, you'd better think about this."

As casually as if he were lighting a cigarette, he dropped the torch into the pile of bodies. Within seconds the dead men's clothing burst into flame.

"You'd better leave, Danny. Unless you want to become part of the bonfire."

"I'm not leaving until you let the woman go, Ned."

At his words a sly look crossed the leader's face. "You mean that's what this is all about? I thought it was revenge for what we did to you. But it isn't, is it? It's the woman." He studied her with new respect, then tightened his grasp before looking up at Nevada. "She's yours?"

"That's right."

The flames had begun to spread, and the stench of burning flesh caused Jade to gag. But neither man made any move to back down.

"Then why not share?" Ned asked. "Didn't we used to share everything?"

"That's what I thought. But then I learned the hard way that the only one sharing was me. When it came to doing time, my friends disappeared and were willing to let me swing from a rope for crimes I didn't even commit. You wanted me to pay with my life for your crimes."

"Now, Danny. You didn't hang. Just did a little time. But it doesn't seem to have hurt you much. As I understand it, you got yourself a little book learning and even found religion. Why, you look fine. Tougher than ever. Now that you're back," Ned said reasonably, "it'll be like it was before. We'll raise a little hell and have ourselves a real good time. Starting with the woman. Tell you what, you can have her first."

Nevada had a glimpse of Jade's eyes, wide with fear and loathing. She'd been pushed to the limit. He felt the last of his control slipping.

His tone hardened. "Like I said, Ned, I'm not interested in sharing with you. You have one chance to live. Let her go. If you don't, I'll have to kill you. It's that simple."

The outlaw went very still, weighing his chances. He knew that there was little time left before the flames reached the rough boards of the ceiling. When that happened, the hut would cave in upon itself, and everyone inside would be trapped. But he knew he had one slim chance to outwit the gunman facing him. Nevada had no way of knowing that he carried a small pistol inside his sleeve. The trick was to seize a moment to aim and fire.

"You always were better'n me with a gun, Danny," he muttered. "But I was meaner. I guess it had to do with that guilty conscience of yours. Hell, I never had a conscience. So I'm going to call your bluff. I don't believe you can shoot me. And to prove it, I'm not even going to draw my weapon. If you kill me, you'll be killing an unarmed man."

He watched with satisfaction as Nevada lowered his weapon.

Flames were licking the toe of Ned's boot. He knew he'd just run out of time. He held Jade in front of him like a shield and started to stretch out his arm.

"Look out!" Jade shouted, before Ned clapped a hand over her mouth, stilling her words of warning.

Jade felt the panic rise to her throat like bile. She was going to be forced to watch Nevada shot before her eyes. Desperate, she twisted to face her captor and yanked her knife from his waistband.

Startled, he reacted instantly, turning the blade so that it sliced savagely into her hand.

She let out a cry as she fought back, plunging it with all her might into his chest.

Ned gave a gasp of surprise before dropping to his knees. "You . . . little . . ."

He lifted his arm, but before he could engage his weapon, a gunshot reverberated through the hut, and he sprawled facedown. His body was instantly engulfed in flames.

"Wrong choice, Ned," came Nevada's voice. "Looks like you'll have to join your friends in hell."

Jade's legs refused to support her. In a state of shock, she started to sink to the floor. But before she could fall, Nevada swept her into his arms and raced through a wall of fire.

Once outside, he continued running until he was far enough away to escape the smell of death. Then he knelt and deposited Jade in the cool grass.

Seeing the river of blood spilling from her wound, he wrapped it with his bandanna.

"I'm sorry about all this," he murmured. "Truly sorry, Jade. But it's over now. Thanks to you. You saved my life, even though by now you must hate me." His words rang with feeling. "I give you my word that I'll do everything in my power to see you safely home."

When he brushed the hair from her eyes, he realized that his promises were in vain. Jade had been forced to deal with more than her tender spirit could accept. The pain of the knife wound and the shock of all she'd been through had sent her spiraling into darkness.

Chapter Eighteen

Jade clung to the last vestiges of sleep. With her eyes still closed she could feel the warmth of morning sunlight kissing her cheek. Somewhere nearby water could be heard spilling over rocks. A chorus of birdsong carried on the breeze.

The feeling of peace was such a contrast to the violence she'd witnessed, she feared it might be a dream.

Her eyes opened and she glanced around in surprise. It was no dream. She was lying on a bedroll in the shelter of a stand of trees. Coffee bubbled over a fire, filling the air with its delicious aroma. A pan of biscuits rested on a nearby rock. And walking toward her, from the direction of a creek, was Nevada, still buttoning his shirt.

He looked clean and refreshed, and as innocent as the preacher she had once thought him to be.

When he was beside her he dropped to his knees. "You're finally awake."

He felt her cringe at his touch, and cursed himself for his clumsiness. She no longer trusted him. And he couldn't blame her. The man she'd seen last night was a stranger to her. As violent as the outlaws who had kidnapped her.

"Are they...?" She swallowed, then tried again. "Are all those gunmen dead?"

He nodded.

"They knew you. He treated you like one of them."

"I was one of them."

He felt her withdraw as surely as if she'd closed a door.

She couldn't voice all the fears in her heart. She tried to tear her gaze from the drops of water that still glistened in his golden hair. It seemed incongruous that this handsome, charming man, who had led an entire town to believe he was a good and noble man of peace, was actually an outlaw. And now she was at his mercy.

As if reading her thoughts, he handed her the little jewel-handled knife. "You'll want this for protection."

"My knife. How did you manage to salvage it?"

"I knew how much it meant to you."

She clutched it firmly in one hand. "How long have I been sleeping?"

"I'd say it's at least midday."

"Midday!" She sat up, and felt her head spin at the sudden movement.

"Easy, now." Nevada brought his arm around her shoulders. Though she stiffened, she didn't have the strength to push away. "You've lost some blood from the wound in your hand. For the rest of the day I think you'd better take it nice and slow."

She waited until the dizziness passed, then asked, "Where are we?"

"The foothills of Dead Man's Mountain. A day's ride from Hanging Tree."

"We'd better get started." She began to toss aside the blankets, but he caught her arm.

"We're not going anywhere," he said firmly, "until you've had a chance to recover from your ordeal."

"It's just a cut. It could have been worse." Even as she spoke the words she felt the sudden flash of fear, and saw again in her mind the horror she'd been forced to witness. She paled as she whispered, "Oh, Nevada, I was so frightened."

"You're not alone. I was scared half to death."

"You?" She shook her head. "I don't think you've ever been afraid of anything."

He gave her a fierce look. "Not for myself. My life is meaningless. I was afraid for you." His look softened as he placed his saddle like a pillow behind her. "After what you've been through, you need to give yourself time."

He felt her acquiesce as she leaned back. "All right. At least I'll wait a little while, until I feel stronger."

It was a start. Though he knew it was too soon for her to trust him, he'd take whatever concessions she was willing to make.

"How is your hand feeling?"

She glanced down at the clean dressings. "It throbs a bit. How bad is it?"

"Bad enough to cause you pain for a few days. But the wound is clean. It'll mend."

He released her hand and busied himself at the fire, filling a plate with biscuits, pouring coffee into a battered tin cup.

When he handed it to her, she managed to eat several bites before she pushed the plate aside and sipped her coffee. Even that small effort drained her.

She lay back in the bedroll and watched as he crossed to a fallen tree and began to chop firewood. With each bite of the ax she heard again in her mind the sound of the gunfire that had echoed through the little hut, and experienced again all the terror in those moments when she'd thought they would all die.

She closed her eyes against the pain of memory. And escaped into sleep.

It was nearly dusk. The last rays of the setting sun cast a crimson glow over the waters of the creek.

Jade sat up, shocked that she had slept the entire day away. But she knew Nevada had been right to insist upon staying. Her strength was restored, as well as her spirit.

She was surprised to see her tapestry valise beside the bedroll. The last she had seen it, it had been somewhere on the stage.

And then the truth dawned. That was how Nevada had known about her abduction. He'd come upon the driver, and had somehow spotted her valise. If he hadn't... She shuddered. If he hadn't recognized it, she would still be in the clutches of those evil men.

She opened the bag and withdrew her belongings, then tossed the blanket aside and got to her feet, peering around for some sign of Nevada. He was nowhere to be seen. Nor was his horse.

She felt a moment of panic before she forced herself to think rationally. He wouldn't have brought her here, only to leave her. Wherever he'd gone, he would return. In the meantime, she knew how she intended to use these precious moments of privacy.

She walked to the creek and dipped a toe in the water. It was refreshingly cool. She was unprepared for the difficulty of functioning with only one good hand, but after laboring for long minutes she was able to shed her gown and step into the water.

Oh, how good it felt to wash away the grime of the trail. She ducked beneath the waves and came up, shaking her head, sending a spray of water dancing around her. Then she swam, slowly, lazily, feeling the tension begin to dissolve.

By the time she stepped from the creek and struggled to pull on a clean gown, she felt as if she had washed away not only the dirt but the touch of her captors, as well.

Shivering, she turned toward the fire. And was stunned to see Nevada astride his horse, watching her.

"Sorry," he called. "I didn't mean to be gone so long. I'd hoped to be back before you woke."

"I've only been awake a little while. Where did you go?"

He slid from his horse and pointed to the carcass of a deer slung across its back. "I thought you needed something more than biscuits if you're going to regain your strength for the ride to Hanging Tree."

Seeing the way she folded her arms over her chest, he slipped out of his jacket and draped it around her. "Here. You're shivering."

Though she said nothing, she felt oddly touched by his gesture. He was being overly solicitous. And at the moment it was exactly what she needed.

As she made her way to the fire, she was aware of the way Nevada watched her. Though he still had the ability to affect her with a simple touch or look, she couldn't forget what she had learned about him in those brief, shocking moments in the hut. She would have to learn to harden her heart.

As the moon rose over the mountain peaks, she sat huddled in the bedroll. Beside her, Nevada roasted venison over the fire.

"How did you come upon my valise on the stage?" she asked softly. "This isn't the way to Nevada."

"I lied to you," he admitted. "I was never heading to Nevada."

There was a prolonged silence before she managed to ask, "Why?"

He heard the pain in that simple word, and knew it had a deeper meaning. He kept his gaze averted. It was easier if he wasn't looking into those big dark eyes, seeing all the doubt and mistrust. "I had to leave San Francisco. It was time for me to confront my past."

"But why did you have to lie to me?"

"I thought it would spare you some pain. I had no right to take... what you were about to offer me."

Her cheeks grew hot. "You knew what I was planning?"

He nodded. "I overheard everything."

She hung her head in shame.

Seeing it, he lowered his voice to a mere whisper and touched a hand to her cheek. "Don't misunderstand. It was everything I wanted. All I'd ever dreamed of, since the first time I saw you. But I knew I had no right to such a gift. You deserve so much better than me, Jade. I realize now that what I did was cowardly. You should have heard the truth about me before I left."

She swallowed. "And what is the truth?"

"I'm not at all the man you think I am."

"And what are you?"

"A loner. A liar. A cheat." He looked away. "I've been on my own for most of my life. In order to survive, I had to grow up fast."

"Why were you alone?" she asked softly. "What happened to your parents?"

"My father died when I was eight. My mother was young, not much more than a kid herself. And the harshness of her life beat her down."

"In what way?"

He shrugged. "In so many ways. I'd find her sitting in a rocker, staring into space. She couldn't seem to rouse herself enough to care for the little ones."

"You had brothers and sisters?"

"Two little sisters. Just babies. They needed a mother, but she just couldn't handle it after my father...after he died. And there was a man..." His jaw clenched. His features hardened. "One day I came home from hunting up our supper and found the cabin empty. I learned from a nearby rancher that she'd taken off with a sweet-talking cowboy."

Jade gasped. Though she wasn't even aware of it, she touched a hand to his arm. "She left an eight-year-old boy to survive alone?"

He shrugged. "I guess I was too much for her to handle. After my father's death I let the anger and rage fill up all the empty spaces inside me." He turned away before adding, "A month or so after my mother and the girls left, Ned came along."

Jade tried to imagine an eight-year-old surviving for a month alone in a little cabin in the wilderness.

"Ned wasn't much more than fifteen or sixteen, but to me he seemed like a seasoned outlaw. He was running with a gang and offered to take me along."

"But you were just a child."

"I told you. I had to grow up fast. Ned convinced me that my only chance to survive was to surround myself with tough outlaws with plenty of guns, or I'd end up dying young like my father. So he and his gang became my family. We crisscrossed the West, staying one step ahead of the law. And in the winter we holed up in that hut."

"So that was how you found us so quickly. You knew where they were taking me."

He nodded.

Jade felt her eyes fill with tears at the life he'd described. "It must have been horrible for you."

He made an attempt to smile, but it fell flat. "It was no Sunday school picnic. But I survived."

"Ned called you Danny."

"Danny is dead," he said harshly. "I buried him when I was eight, and took the name Nevada. With Ned as my teacher, I became an expert with a gun."

"But you weren't like those outlaws," she said with a shudder. "You could never be like them."

He turned on her with eyes blazing. "Don't try to make me something I'm not, Jade. I ran with a gang. I've broken every rule of God and man. I told you. I'm a thief and a cheat and a murderer."

"You aren't," she said hotly. "I know you. You aren't a killer."

As gently as he could manage he said, "I've killed men, Jade. You saw me shoot them without a backward glance whenever they threatened me or someone I cared about."

She put her hand over his. "But that was self-defense. You didn't go out looking for them. It was kill or be killed."

He allowed her hand to remain there, warming his. It was a simple act, but it touched a chord deep inside him. "They're still dead because of me. In the eyes of the law that makes me a killer." He busied himself by filling a plate with biscuits and sizzling meat, and handing it to her. When she met his eyes his lips curved into a wry smile.

"Too bad you weren't the lawman who finally brought me to trial. It might have gone a lot easier for me."

"Trial?"

He nodded and looked away. "The sheriff wanted to make an example of me, and have me hung for the crimes committed by the Garland Gang. The judge took the word of witnesses who said I'd stepped in to save their lives whenever Ned got too violent. Except in self-defense, I never shot a man. So he let me off with five years in prison."

She blanched.

Seeing her reaction, he said more gently, "It probably saved my life. I had five years to think about where I was headed. And I realized that I'd wasted half my life being angry about something that was over and done with. Nothing would ever bring my father back. I decided that when I got out I could repeat my mistakes, or make a better life for myself."

"And that's when you became the Reverend Wade Weston?"

"I tried," he said softly. "God knows I tried. And it felt good to have the respect of people. But the old ways are hard to forget. Sometimes I felt helpless carrying a Bible instead of a gun. Especially when I learned that Ned and the gang were back plying their trade. The first time they attacked you, I instinctively reached for a gun."

"It was you!" Her eyes grew wide. "You were my guardian angel."

He gave a grim smile and stared into the flames of the fire. "Some guardian angel. I couldn't even acknowledge what I'd done." He turned his head away. "The people of Hanging Tree deserve better than me. That's what I intend to tell them when I get to town."

She set her plate aside and clutched his arm, her voice trembling with indignation. "You're wrong about the townspeople. They love you. You've made a difference in their lives. Once they hear the truth, they'll welcome you back."

"If you believe that, Jade, you must believe in miracles. The good people of Hanging Tree will try to nail my hide to the wall of Durfee's Mercantile after they learn the truth about me.''

"Then why bother going back?''

He got to his feet. "Because I owe them that much. Call it the last of my...unfinished business in Hanging Tree."

Jade watched as he strode away and blended into the darkness beyond the circle of firelight.

The food on her plate grew cold as she stared up at the stars and thought about all that he'd told her. It was almost too much to take in at one time.

Feeling weary beyond belief, she crawled into the bedroll. Almost instantly she fell into a deep, dreamless sleep.

Jade stared at the darkened sky. She had no way of knowing how long she'd been asleep. The heavens, black as midnight, were awash with millions of stars.

Nevada's words echoed through her mind. *You were all I'd ever dreamed of, since the first time I saw you. But I knew I had no right to such a gift. You deserve so much better than me.*

She sat up, shoving the tangles from her eyes. How could she have been so blind?

Of all the things she'd learned about Nevada's past, only one mattered. His leaving hadn't been a rejection of her, but rather an affirmation that he didn't think himself worthy of her love. But he wanted her. And had since the first time he'd seen her.

And despite everything she had learned about his past, she still loved him. Desperately.

It was time for some honesty of her own.

Nevada sat by the fire, his back against the trunk of a gnarled tree, his thoughts dark and tormented. Smoke from his cigar curled like a wreath over his head.

It hadn't been as tough as he'd imagined. But then, he hadn't been as honest as he'd intended. Odd, he thought, how the best of plans...

He turned at the soft footfall, then groaned inwardly as Jade dropped to her knees beside him. She looked like a vision he'd conjured out of his tortured needs.

"You should be sleeping," he said a little too gruffly.

"I was." She knew her voice sounded breathless, but she couldn't help it. She wanted to act quickly, before she had time to change her mind. "Something woke me."

He glanced around, his hand going to his gun. "I didn't hear anything."

"It wasn't a sound. It was a voice in my mind."

His eyes narrowed slightly. "I don't get it."

She gave him a smile so dazzling it had his heart constricting. "You said you overheard what I told Aunt Lily. About planning to...seduce you."

"We've been through all this." If he wasn't so frustrated, he might see the humor in this situation. As it was, he felt only anger.

He caught her roughly by the upper arms and stood, dragging her to her feet. Though she was surprised by his sudden movement, she held her ground.

"You said you wanted me. And have since the first time you saw me."

"That's enough, Jade. Go on back to your bedroll." He turned away from her and, needing to hide his feelings, drew deeply on his cigar.

"Have I done something to change your mind?" she asked softly.

"It isn't anything you've done. It's me. It's... everything. My past. My future. Hell," he said through gritted teeth, "I have no future."

"I'm not interested in your past or your future. All I care about is here, now." She placed a hand on his arm and felt him flinch and draw away as though burned.

Fear clogged her throat, and she thought about retreating. But then she caught sight of his proud profile. Flaring nostrils. Jutting chin. Heaving chest. Heaving? Could it be that the brave, tough gunman was fighting a battle with himself? Over her?

That knowledge made her bolder than ever.

She brought her hand to his shoulder. "I love you, Nevada. I know I shouldn't. But I can't help the way I feel about you. And I think you have some feeling for me, as well."

Love. That simple word had him stunned and reeling. He'd been prepared for any argument but that. If she'd said she wanted to learn the ways of men and women, he would have found the courage to walk away. If she'd tried to be cute or coy, playful or demanding, he could have resisted.

But love. Simple, honest love. It was his most basic need. One he had so long been denied.

Still, for her sake, he had to try to deny it.

He turned to face her, his features deliberately bland. "Weren't you listening when Lily warned you about the perils of love?"

She reacted as though he'd slapped her. It tore at him to hurt her, but it was for her own good.

"You saw what it did to your father and mother. Even the love they felt for you couldn't bring them together as a family. What if we repeat their mistake? Is that what you want, Jade? A child who spends a lifetime wishing for a life that can never be?"

When she remained silent he knew, with a heavy heart, that he'd won. For good measure he added, "Now go back to your bedroll and get some sleep. You'll need it. We're leaving for Hanging Tree at first light."

He turned away, closed his eyes and listened to the slight rustling of her gown. In the silence that followed he lifted his cigar to his lips, inhaled deeply, then tossed it on the fire and turned.

She was standing very still, watching him.

"I thought..." he began.

She touched a finger to his lips. "You thought you had succeeded in driving me away. That's what you wanted, isn't it? To save me from myself?"

His voice was a low whisper of anguish. "For God's sake, leave me, Jade, now, before it's too late."

"It's already too late." She stood on tiptoe and brought her mouth to his.

He absorbed the shock of her kiss. His whole world was tilting, and he couldn't seem to right it. Still, he had to try.

He caught her roughly by the shoulders and held her a little away. "You don't know what you're doing. This isn't an elegant pleasure palace with perfumed sheets and feather beds. There are no servants to do your bidding, or Lee Yin to help you when you find yourself in over your head." When she opened her mouth to protest, he muttered, "And be warned. I'm not a gentleman. I won't settle for a quick tumble in the grass. I'll want more than you're prepared to give." She saw the passion that blazed in his eyes before he carefully banked it. "I'll want everything, Jade. Everything, do you understand? Now get out of here, before we both have to wake up in the morning with regrets."

Instead of turning away when he released her, she surprised him by wrapping her arms around his neck and lifting her mouth to his. "I won't leave. And you can't make me go."

It was the final straw. He had no strength left to refuse her.

As his lips covered hers he muttered thickly, "Understand, then. I want it all."

Chapter Nineteen

His hands were almost bruising as he gripped her shoulders and drove her backward against the tree. His kisses weren't gentle. With lips and teeth and tongue, he took. He demanded. He devoured. His breath was hot as it mingled with hers in a moan of impatience.

He feasted on her lips, drawing out every flavor, every exotic taste. When he lifted his head they were both gasping for breath. His hands fumbled with the fasteners at her neck until the silk was shredded. He took no notice of the torn fabric as he dragged his lips over her throat. But even as his mouth brought her pleasure, his hands were exploring, moving aside her skirt until he found her, already hot and moist.

She reacted to his frenzied assault like a frightened doe.

"No. Wait." Dragging air into her lungs, she pushed against him.

He lifted his head, and she could see his eyes, glazed with a dangerous light. "I warned you I wasn't a gentleman. Having second thoughts?"

She shook her head, struggling for breath. "It's just... I need a moment to think."

"It's too late for that. Don't think." He lifted a handful of hair from her neck and brushed his lips over the tender flesh, sending tremors skittering along her spine. And all the while his hands continued to weave their magic until her body was vibrating like a plucked harp. "Just feel, Jade. Feel."

He watched her eyes as he drove her to the first sudden, shocking peak.

She couldn't speak. Not when his lips and fingertips were doing such amazing things to her. Her body hummed with strange new sensations, but still he gave her no time to recover.

He ran nibbling kisses down her throat, across her shoulder. When her gown got in the way he tore it roughly aside to bare her flesh to his lips.

Though she'd been caught unawares by his reaction, the truth was, his ruthlessness excited her. She brought her arms around his waist, tugging at his shirt, eager to explore him as he was exploring her. His skin was damp, hot with the fever that drove him.

He shrugged aside his clothes and tore away the rest of her gown until they were standing, damp flesh to damp flesh.

Her voice was ragged and trembling. "I can't believe this is happening. I have no pride left. You've managed to make me forget everything my tutor ever taught me."

"I won't be satisfied until the only heart you feel is mine." He dragged her against him until she could feel the thundering of his heartbeat inside her own chest. "And the only thing you taste is me." He took the kiss deeper, until she drank in the dark, dangerous taste of him. "And the only man you see is me."

With a sigh she allowed her lids to flutter closed. Outlined in a red mist of passion was his image, imprinted indelibly on her mind. On her heart. On her soul.

"There's only you," she murmured on a moan of pleasure. "Oh, Nevada, only you."

"And you're the only woman I'll ever want or need." With his hand tangled in her hair he drew her head back while his other hand skimmed her body. His mouth plundered hers until they were both struggling for breath.

The need for her was so overpowering, he had to call on all his willpower to keep from taking her. There was a beast inside him, clawing its way out, driving him unmercifully. But this was her first time, he cautioned himself. There was so little he could give her. But he could give her this. Pleasure beyond just this night. And memories to last a lifetime.

Moment by painful moment he managed to rein in his out-of-control passion, so that he could take the time she deserved.

With his hands on her shoulders he held her a little away and rested his forehead against hers while he took several deep drafts of air.

"What is it?" she whispered. "Have I done something wrong?"

"Oh, Jade." He combed his fingers through her hair and stared deeply into her eyes. "You couldn't do anything wrong if you tried. You're so right. So incredibly right." He ran nibbling kisses over her upturned face, pausing to brush his lips over her eyelids, her cheeks, the tip of her nose. "But I want this to be special for you."

"How could it not be special when it's with you, Nevada?"

Her words touched him so deeply, he felt his breath hitch in his throat. He lifted her hands to his lips, pressing a kiss to each palm. Then, still holding her hands, he drew her down until they were kneeling in the cool grass, with only their discarded clothes as a cushion.

He felt a welling of tenderness as he enclosed her in the circle of his embrace and sought her mouth. She gave it willingly, eagerly, as she twined her arms around his neck.

The sounds of the night washed over them. The lapping of water in the creek. The chirp and hum of insects. The call of a night bird. The sighing of the wind in the trees. All of these things helped to gentle the raging passion in him as he lost himself in the wonder of her.

With great care he laid her down and trailed hot, wet kisses along her throat, across her collarbone, to her breast.

Pleasure. Jade had never experienced such pleasure. She lay, calm and still in his arms, trusting him to lead the way.

He sensed her trust and thrilled to it. It was the highest compliment she could pay him, knowing that she'd been taught to trust no one but herself.

As his hands and lips moved over her, her body arched, tight with need. She had become a mass of nerve endings. And Nevada instinctively knew every one.

Heat. Her blood surged like molten lava. She was so hot, it was an effort to breathe. Even the damp grass couldn't cool her overheated flesh. And still he took her higher, then higher still, keeping release just out of reach, until she moaned and writhed and cried out his name.

Her arousal fueled his own. He looked into her eyes, glazed with desire. The fragrance of exotic flowers and spices filled him, until all he could taste, all he could breathe, was her.

"Tell me," he whispered fiercely. "Tell me that you want me."

She was beyond wanting. Beyond words. She had slipped into a world of such deep feeling, pleasure actually bordered on pain.

"I want..." She swallowed and tried again. "You. Only you. Oh, Nevada, love me. Now."

Feeling his tenuous grasp on sanity slipping away, he moved over her, taking her with a savageness that had them both gasping. But when he tried to slow down, to give her time, she wrapped herself around him, taking him beyond the point of return. She began to move with him, matching his strength, his rhythm, until they felt as though they'd broken free of earth. It was the most incredible feeling as they soared through the heavens. And at last touched the stars in a blinding flash of light.

They lay still, their bodies slick, their heartbeats still racing out of control. Slowly, ever so slowly, they drifted back to earth.

Jade's breathing was shallow, her mind still humming with all she'd discovered. So this was the passion that men and women experienced. The passion that had fueled the imaginations of the artists and poets of her mother's land for centuries.

She felt tears spring to her eyes. This was what her father and mother had tried to fight. And when they could no longer deny it, this was the bond that held them, though they led separate lives.

For Jade the knowledge was stunning. And devastating. How could her parents have remained apart for even one night when they shared something this powerful, this compelling?

Tasting the salt of her tears, Nevada felt his heart stop. He lifted his thumbs to the corners of her eyes as he growled between clenched teeth, "I can't believe I took you like a savage, right here on the ground. I feel like the lowest—"

"That isn't why I'm crying." She sniffed, struggling to stem the flow. "It's just so...wonderful. I was thinking about my parents. It must have broken their hearts to be apart."

Relieved that he wasn't the cause of her weeping, Nevada felt his own heart begin to beat once more. He rolled to his side and drew her into the circle of his arms, loving the way she curled herself contentedly against him.

They remained silent for long moments, each lost in private thoughts.

But when she shivered, he broke the silence by murmuring against her temple, "The night's growing cold. I'd better get you into a bedroll."

As he started to get up she touched a hand to his arm to stop him. "I don't want you to leave me. Even for a moment. I know a better way to keep warm."

He glanced down at her with a look of surprise and amusement. "Why, Miss Jewel. Whatever are you talking about?"

"I believe it's called...cuddling."

"And what would you know about such things?"

"A notorious outlaw was kind enough to share his vast experience in . . . certain areas in which I was deficient."

"How generous of him." He lifted a strand of her hair and watched as it sifted through his fingers.

"He's a very generous man. And now I'd like to return the favor." She sat up and with her finger traced the curve of his brow, the hollow of his cheek, the outline of his lips, all the while watching his eyes. "I've wanted to do this for such a long time."

"Too bad you didn't tell me sooner. I'd have been happy to oblige."

She gave him a mysterious smile and continued tracing his firm jaw, the slope of his shoulder.

"You'd better be careful," he muttered thickly, "or that outlaw you mentioned might have even more things he'd like to share."

She seemed intrigued. "Is that possible? I mean . . . so soon?"

"If he's as notorious as you say, I think there's a good chance of it. Especially if you keep touching him like this."

She pressed her lips to his throat and heard his little intake of breath. That only made her bolder. She surprised him by tracing her lips down the line of red-gold hair that matted his chest. When she brought her lips lower, he gave a growl of pleasure, deep in his throat.

Catching her roughly by the shoulders, he hauled her into his arms. Against her mouth he whispered,

"I warned you. Now you're going to have to suffer the consequences."

"Promise?" she said with a laugh.

His tongue circled her ear, then thrust inside. "I never promise what I can't deliver."

She shivered. Her laughter died as his lips began an intimate exploration of her body. Without warning she found herself tumbling once more with him into a world of passion. A world of dark, desperate desire. A world where only lovers can go.

Nevada lay watching the woman asleep in his arms. Sometime during the night he had managed to carry her to his bedroll. But neither of them had given much thought to sleep.

Their lovemaking had been by turns fierce and gentle, at times as playful as children, at other times so darkly passionate they came together with all the frenzy of a thunderstorm. Through it all, Jade had been a source of constant delight.

He watched her now as the sunrise cast her lovely face in light and shadow. She was so beautiful she took his breath away. She was an innocent and a temptress. A child and a woman. A lover and a friend.

She made him achingly aware of all the things he'd always known were beyond his grasp. Marriage. Family. Roots. The pain was so sudden, he closed his eyes against it.

If he could, he would hold back the dawn, so that
they could stay here forever, safely sheltered from the
civilized world. Civilized. He frowned. He much
preferred this wilderness paradise to harsh reality.
But sooner or later, civilization would have to be
faced.

By now, Jade's family would have received word
that she was returning to Texas. When the stage
didn't arrive, they would think the worst. He had to
spare them any more worry. Still, the desire to remain here was tempting. Here they had no one to
please but each other. In Hanging Tree they would
incur the wrath of everyone. He didn't mind for
himself. He'd made his choices, most of them wrong,
a long time ago. But Jade was different. She was already vulnerable to attacks by the townspeople because of the Golden Dragon. She didn't need the
added burden of being linked to an infamous outlaw.

"Is that hunger I see?" She touched a finger to the
little frown line between his brows. "Or are you
worried about something?"

"Just thinking."

"Sounds ominous." She gave a throaty laugh. In
an attempt to lighten his mood, she pressed her lips
to his neck and ran feathery kisses across his shoulder. When that didn't bring the expected smile, she
lifted a finger and began to trace the furrow in his
brow.

He looked down to find her watching him with a look of concern. Instantly his frown disappeared. Catching her finger, he dipped it into his mouth, nipping lightly. With a smile she traced the fullness of his lips, then brought her finger to her own mouth and tasted him, as he had once done.

She saw the way his amber eyes darkened with sudden passion.

"Um-hmm," she muttered. "I thought so. Hunger."

"But not for food," he breathed against her mouth a moment before his lips claimed hers. "For you."

And then there was no need for words. They slipped once more into their warm cocoon, insulated from the world outside. A place where there were no angry words or violent outlaws. A place where they were safe. And thoroughly satisfied. And completely loved.

"I don't want another bandage on this hand," Jade complained as Nevada cut a strip of linen and began to wrap it firmly around her cut.

She was still lying naked in the bedroll. Nevada, wearing nothing but a blanket, had little drops of water in his hair from his morning bath.

"Don't argue. You need a clean dressing until the wound is completely healed."

"But I wanted to take a bath in the creek and wash my hair." She glanced up at him through a fringe of lashes as he finished tying the linen.

She was shamelessly flirting. And he loved her for it.

"Is that all that's bothering you?" His eyes gleamed and she saw the hint of laughter in his smile. "Why didn't you say so?" Before she could respond he tossed aside his blanket, picked up her fragrant soap and scooped her into his arms.

"What are you doing?" she demanded as he waded into the water.

"I'm going to wash your hair. And...anything else you'd like."

He set her in the water, taking care to keep her freshly bandaged hand high enough to remain dry. "Just sit here in the shallows. I'll do all the work," he murmured as he began running the soap through her tangles.

She closed her eyes as he gently massaged her scalp. "You have strong fingers."

"Umm." He took his time, clearly enjoying himself. "But they've never been used for such... rewarding work before. I used to wonder what your hair felt like," he muttered as he worked up a lather. "And now I know. It's as soft as a web spun with dew. And as beautiful."

She felt herself blushing. "Can this be the man who calls himself an outlaw? Are you sure you aren't a poet?"

He laughed. "Don't tell anyone, but I did read a little poetry in jail. And I often wondered how a man could carry on so about a woman's lips. Or hair. But when I saw you the night of your birthday at the Golden Dragon, I understood. Do you have any idea how long your image remained with me on the trail, warming my nights, fueling my dreams?"

At his admission, her eyes widened. "You are a poet. Or a shameless flatterer."

"Maybe I'm both. Now close your eyes," he said as he pressed her back against his arm and rinsed the soap from her hair.

She did as she was told. "Umm. This is heavenly."

"I'm glad you like it." He moved the soap across her shoulders, down her throat, over her breasts.

Her eyes snapped open. But his hand had already moved lower, across her stomach, along her thigh.

"Nevada." Her voice was little more than a purr of pleasure. She brought her hands to his chest and water lapped gently around them.

"Your hand..." he began, but it was already too late. The bandage was soaked.

Neither of them seemed to care as they came together in the slow, leisurely ritual of love.

"Why do we have to go?" With one hand Jade rinsed their plate and cup in the creek while Nevada rolled up their blankets and tied them behind the saddle.

"I told you. Your family will be worried about you."

"But it's too soon." She hated whining. Hated being cross with him. But with each passing minute she had grown increasingly cranky. She felt like a petulant child.

Suddenly inspired, she held up her hand. Though the pain was minimal, she would use any excuse to prolong the time of their departure. "My hand will be even better tomorrow."

He didn't say a word. How could he criticize her when he was raging against the same things? Instead he crossed the distance that separated them and dragged her against him. The kiss was long, slow, intimate. Then he lifted her in his arms and settled her in the saddle, before pulling himself up behind her and catching up the reins.

Without a word they turned away from the place that had become their haven. And started toward home.

Chapter Twenty

It was nearly dusk when they rode into Hanging Tree. Though the sight of the two of them sharing a horse caused many an eyebrow to be lifted, not a single resident of the town called out a greeting. Most turned away quickly, avoiding their eyes.

Jade and Nevada exchanged glances before riding on in silence.

A short time later they crested a hill and saw the lights of the ranch house in the distance. Jade's heart leapt to her throat. Home. There had been a time, during her capture, that she had feared she'd never see this ranch again, or the beloved faces of her sisters. But now that she was here, she had an even greater fear. That somehow her return home meant the loss of this man who had captured her heart.

Even as they drew near, Jade could feel Nevada withdrawing from her.

"Take a few days to rest." His voice was barely a whisper in her ear as he slowed his horse to a walk. "You shouldn't come into town for a while."

"Are you trying to frighten me?"

He halted the stallion and slid to the ground. "Just trying to save you a little discomfort. You saw how the people reacted when they saw us together."

She clung to him after he helped her dismount. "I want you to spend the night here, Nevada. In the morning we'll face the townspeople together."

They both looked up as the door was thrown open and Diamond, Pearl, Ruby and Carmelita came running onto the porch. They were alternately laughing and weeping as they approached the couple.

"Jade. Oh, Jade," Diamond shouted. "Thank heaven you're all right."

"We've been so worried," Pearl cried. "Adam and Cal and the wranglers have been out searching for hours. We'll have to send Cookie with the news that you're safely home."

"You look—" Ruby studied her sister with a critical eye "—different. What's happened to you?"

Before Jade could think of a response, Carmelita caught up her hand. "You have been hurt."

"It's just a cut. It's healing nicely."

With her hand beneath Jade's elbow, Carmelita began urging her up the steps. "Oh, Señorita Jade. You will eat. And then you will tell us everything. Reverend Weston, you will join us?"

"No. I have to get to town. I have ... unfinished business to take care of."

Jade pulled free and turned. "You don't have to face them so soon. At least stay the night."

"You know I can't."

Seeing the looks that passed between the two, Diamond said, "The town gossips have been having a fine time discussing the disappearance of both of you. There have even been silly rumors that you two arranged to meet in another town."

"I feared as much. The townspeople will want a meeting," Nevada said tiredly. "When it's over, Jade, I expect they'll order me to leave as quickly as possible." He pulled himself into the saddle.

She ran down the steps and caught his sleeve. "If they order you to leave, I'm going with you."

He reached down and for the briefest moment touched her hand. "You know I ride alone."

She held tightly to him. "Not anymore. Not after what we've shared." She saw the closed look on his face and her tone became pleading. "We could have a future together. I don't care what others think."

He released her hand and clutched the reins. When their eyes met, his were as hard as flint. Whatever he'd felt for her had been carefully locked away in his heart. Now that she was safely home, he was preparing himself, and her, for the emptiness that was certain to follow. "You'd better start caring. I warn you, Jade, I know what it is to be an outcast. I won't allow it to happen to you. I couldn't live with myself if I were to cause you to face an angry mob."

"You didn't cause any of this. Loving you was my choice. Mine," she said fiercely.

The four women who stood listening reacted with shock. Love? Their sister had been gone only a few weeks. When had she learned to love the town preacher?

As he wheeled his mount she called, "I warn you, Nevada. I won't be separated from you."

He rode away without a backward glance.

Watching him, she realized that her words had been an echo of the very things her father had said to her mother. And yet, for all the love they had shared, her parents had lived—and died—apart.

Oh, honorable Father, she thought as she struggled to hold back her tears, *is this to be my legacy? Must I repeat your mistake and find myself forever separated from the only one I'll ever love?*

She struggled to compose herself. When horse and rider dipped below a ridge and disappeared from view, she turned. And found Diamond, Pearl and Ruby studying her in silence.

Seeing the tears that shimmered on her lashes, they gathered around her with hugs and kisses.

"We expected a celebration," Diamond whispered. "Instead, we find you grieving. Can you tell us what happened?"

"Give me a minute." Jade accepted the delicately embroidered handkerchief Pearl held out to her and wiped her tears. Then, following the others inside, she took her place at the table. It was a somber little group that gathered around. But slowly, painfully, with many interruptions, she told them everything.

"He was very brave," Pearl said.

"Your guardian angel," Ruby added with a smile.

"And you love him." Diamond's voice was hushed with awe.

Jade nodded. "But when the townspeople learn of his past, his future here will be over."

The sisters glanced at each other, acknowledging the truth of that statement. Diamond spoke for all of them. "Lavinia and the others will never accept a former outlaw as their preacher."

Jade pushed away from the table, unable to eat a thing.

"You must rest now," Diamond said firmly.

"I don't want to rest." Jade held back as the others started toward the stairs. "I'll never be able to close my eyes knowing what tomorrow will bring."

"You must try," Pearl said. "For Reverend Weston's sake, as well as your own."

They walked with her up the stairs. At the door to her bedroom they embraced her, and fervently prayed that their love and support would be enough to sustain her through whatever was to come.

Hours later, after Diamond and Adam had returned to their own ranch, and Pearl and Cal and their boys had started out for their little home on the banks of Poison Creek, Ruby climbed the stairs to her bed. At the door to Jade's room she paused and listened. Hearing no sound from within, she gave a little sigh of relief and hurried off to bed.

What she didn't know was that the object of her concern had let herself out the upstairs window. And was already halfway to town.

Jade held the lantern aloft and stared around. Over the door the word *Golden* had been painted in gold leaf. The rest would probably be completed tomorrow. Inside, the rooms smelled of paint and wood shavings. The walls and floors were bare, except for some tools left by the workmen.

She climbed the stairs to the upper floor, to the room she'd selected to be her bedroom. She would furnish it with a sumptuous feather bed, and satin sheets. For Nevada, she thought, fighting the panic that fluttered in the pit of her stomach. He would be here to share it. He had to be. For she would accept no other.

She walked to the window and looked down at the sleeping town. What if they ordered Nevada to leave? She wouldn't think about it. Couldn't. She turned away, blinking back tears.

As she descended the stairs, she stopped in midstride at the sight of someone in the circle of lantern light.

"Who is it? Who is there?" Her hand went to the knife at her waist.

"Birdie. Birdie Bidwell," came a faltering voice. The little girl stepped forward, keeping her eyes downcast.

"You gave me quite a scare, Birdie."

"Sorry, ma'am. I heard you were back in town. When I saw the light, I figured it was you. I . . . need to talk to you."

"Now? In the middle of the night? Why didn't you wait until morning, Birdie?"

The girl swallowed. "I didn't want anyone to know about . . . what I wanted to ask you. You see . . ." She was twisting the end of her tattered shawl around and around her finger, keeping her gaze averted. "Times are real hard, Miss Jewel. Mama says she can't let me go to Miss Pearl's school anymore, 'cause she needs me to work. Only there isn't any work in town, 'cept sometimes when Mrs. Potter needs me at the boardinghouse. And so I thought . . ." She licked her lips and forced herself to go on. "I thought maybe you could let me work here."

Jade tried to hide her shock. "Do you know what the women will be expected to do here?"

"Yes'm. Sort of."

"How old are you, Birdie?"

"Thirteen, ma'am. But folks say I'm big for my age."

"Thirteen. And what do you think your folks would say if they knew you were thinking of working here?"

"I expect they'd be shamed by it. They're good folks. Decent folks. But I'm desperate, Miss Jewel." Tears filled her eyes, and her lower lip began quivering. "I overheard my pa tell my ma that there was no way he could hold us together much longer. He's—" she took a deep breath and said the rest on a rush of air, to hide the pain "—thinking of turning me out to fend for myself. And I'm scared, Miss Jewel. I don't know anything 'cept cooking and cleaning and book learning. And no one around here has any need for that. They're all just barely getting by as it is." The tears fell freely now, and she swiped at her eyes with the back of her hand, making her look even more like a child.

Jade felt her heart breaking for the girl. As she started to put her arms around her, Birdie resisted. "You'll get your fine, elegant gown all dirty if you touch me. And my tears will leave stains on your silk shawl."

"You let me worry about that," Jade said, gathering the girl close.

She held Birdie while the tears flowed and her body shook with sobs. When at last the bout of weeping ended, Jade handed her a clean handkerchief.

Composing herself, Birdie said, "Working here wouldn't be so terrible. Look at you. No matter what folks say about you, you're a fine, elegant lady." The girl blew her nose. "Mrs. Thurlong and the others say you're the object of men's lust. And that many a man has abandoned his responsibilities to his wife and children because of women like you." She lowered her gaze. "But I don't care if they say the same about me, as long as I have a place where..." Her eyes filled again, and the tears started trickling down her cheeks. "Where I can earn my keep. Where I can belong. Miss Pearl says I'm a fast learner. You could teach me to do... whatever I have to, in order to be a woman like you."

A woman like you.

Jade thought of Lily, agreeing to an arrangement with her married lover because it was all that she could ever hope for. And now this innocent was willing to embrace the same stigma. To forgo the chance for marriage and children in order to survive the harshness of her life.

Jade held the girl close again and allowed her to cry her heart out. When at last she lifted her head, Jade smoothed the hair from Birdie's face and gazed into her red-rimmed eyes.

"Don't worry about earning your keep," she murmured. "You'll always have a job with me, Birdie."

"I will? You'll teach me... all I have to know?"

"It's the least I can do," Jade said softly, "since you just taught me something I needed to know."

"I did? What was that, Miss Jewel?"

Jade gave her a sad, mysterious look. "Something I've needed to learn for a long time." She turned the girl toward the door. "Now go home and get some sleep, Birdie. And don't mention your little visit. It will have to be our secret.''

''Yes'm.'' At the door she paused to say something more, but Jade had already turned away. In profile she looked sad and pensive. And deep in thought.

As the news spread that Reverend Wade Weston had spent the night at Millie Potter's boardinghouse, half the town seemed to congregate out front, led by Lavinia Thurlong and Gladys Witherspoon. Everyone, it seemed, was itching for a confrontation.

''What a coincidence.'' Lavinia's eyes looked hard enough to shoot bullets as she addressed the crowd. ''Reverend Wade Weston returns to town, after an absence of some weeks, on the same horse as the proprietress of the Golden Dragon. I'd like to hear him deny he was with that shameless hussy.''

A murmur rippled through the crowd. It grew to a roar when they spotted the object of their wrath striding out the door. The Reverend Weston, wearing a crisp white shirt and perfectly tailored dark suit, didn't have the look of a beaten man. In fact, he looked more handsome and charming than ever.

To make matters worse, Jade and her sisters arrived in her fancy carriage at the same time.

''You're not welcome in this town anymore, Reverend Weston,'' Lavinia said. ''Good, decent folks like us deserve someone better to minister to our souls than the likes of you. You have a nerve, preaching from the Good Book, and all the while dallying with a...fallen woman." Seeing that her friends and neighbors were nodding in agreement, she grew bolder. "Hanging is too good for the likes of you. Get on your horse and ride out of here." She turned in the direction of Jade and her sisters. "And take your harlot with you."

Diamond, Pearl and Ruby formed a protective ring around Jade, who surprised them by pushing herself free to stand alone. "My sisters are not a party to this," she said, hoping to distance them from her shame. "The fault is mine alone."

Hearing her words, Nevada moved quickly to divert attention from Jade to himself. He shocked the townspeople by saying softly, "Mrs. Thurlong is absolutely right. All of you deserve better. That's why I've come back. To admit the truth."

"That'll be a change," Lavinia said tartly. "We've called a town meeting in the back of Durfee's Mercantile. Let's see to it quickly, so we can send you on your way and the town of Hanging Tree can once again hold its head high." She turned on her heel, with the rest of the townspeople following.

The crowd swept along, with Nevada in their midst. Jade hurried to her carriage and turned the team to follow. By the time she and her sisters entered the mercantile, all the seats had been taken. They were forced to stand in the back of the room.

From her position Jade could see so many familiar faces. Birdie Bidwell was there, along with her parents. The girl hung her head, avoiding Jade's eyes.

Millie Potter sat with her daughters, April, May and June. Crowded in beside them was Farley Duke and his employees from the sawmill. Though they had gladly taken Jade's money to construct her building, and had greeted her warmly every day, they now looked the other way when they caught sight of her.

Nevada stood alone facing the angry mob.

"There's no point in wasting time," Lavinia shouted above the din. "I say we order Reverend Weston to confess his sins and then banish him from our town forever."

Deputy Arlo Spitz voiced his approval. "Then we can get down to the really important things, like going after the Garland Gang that's been killing innocent ranchers in these parts."

"Now, just a minute," Rufus Durfee cried. Since the meeting was being held in his store, the crowd was forced to pay attention. "Let's have some kind of order." He pounded a hammer on a countertop for attention. "As I see it, this is a simple case of charging the reverend here with sleeping with a woman of ill repute. Does anybody have any proof of those charges?"

"They left town at the same time. Weeks later they returned on the same horse." Lavinia stuck her hands on her hips and turned toward her neighbors with a snicker. "I don't know about the rest of you, but that's proof enough for me."

At the coarse comments that followed, Jade felt her face flame. But she held her head high, refusing to give in to the feeling of shame that washed over her. This had all been her fault. Now Nevada couldn't even deny their accusations.

"I guess we'll ask the reverend here to speak his piece. Then we'll take a vote of the citizens." Rufus rapped his hammer a couple of times for silence.

Before Nevada could begin, however, the marshal strode forward. His face bore a stubble of dark growth, and his clothes were still covered with the dust of the trail. His look was grim as he said loudly, "I'm happy to report that the gang of outlaws that's been terrorizing the countryside won't be bothering any of our citizens anymore."

A cheer went up from the crowd.

"Thank you, Marshal," Lavinia said fervently. "I'm sure I speak for the entire town when I say how proud we are that you could rid us of that plague."

"Actually, Mrs. Thurlong, it wasn't my doing," he admitted. "Reverend Weston told me where I'd find the bodies."

"Bodies?" The crowd grew animated, eager for details.

"I think I'd better ask Miss Jade Jewel to tell you about her experience at the hands of the gang. And how she was rescued."

As one, the assembled townspeople turned to stare at the young woman. Their hostility was a living, palpable thing that seemed to assault her in waves.

"She doesn't look any the worse for her experience," one of the men called.

"Maybe she enjoyed being taken by a gang of outlaws," said another.

The remarks, some whispered, others hurled in anger, were cruel and cutting.

Diamond, whose curses could curl the beard of a seasoned wrangler, managed a few loud retorts before she grabbed her sister's hand. "Don't dignify this meeting with your presence another minute, Jade. Come on. Let's go home."

"No." Jade pulled her hand free. With quiet dignity she lifted the hem of her gown and walked to the front of the room to stand beside Nevada.

The crowd fell deathly silent.

"I think it only fair to give you what you came here for," she said softly. "The truth about what happened between Reverend Weston and me."

Chapter Twenty-One

Jade prayed her voice would not betray her inner turmoil. If the crowd hoped to hear sordid details of a tryst, they would be disappointed. But if what they truly wanted was the truth, she would give it to them.

She swallowed, then, as simply as possible, she told about the attack on her stage, the savage murder of the driver, and her abduction.

"It was Reverend Weston who saved me. If he hadn't recognized my valise on the stage and followed the trail of those villains, I wouldn't be here today."

"That doesn't explain how the preacher happened to be on the trail in the first place," Lavinia said. "Or how a man of the cloth would be carrying a gun. There's a whole lot here we haven't been told."

"You're right, Mrs. Thurlong." Nevada stepped forward, eager to deflect their anger from Jade. "I promised you the truth. And that's what I intend to give you, without holding anything back. You see, the truth is, I used to run with that band of outlaws known as the Garland Gang."

The crowd erupted into chaos, with shouting, cursing. Several men in the room drew their pistols and aimed them at Nevada, until the marshal held up his hands for attention.

"There'll be no shooting in this assembly," he shouted. "The reverend isn't even wearing a gun belt. I'll arrest the first man who doesn't follow my orders and holster his gun immediately."

With muttered complaints, the men did as they were told.

When the crowd grew quiet the marshal said, "Go ahead, Reverend."

"As I said, I was part of a gang." Nevada waited until the murmuring ended. "What's more, I served five years in prison for crimes I committed while I was with them."

This brought even more shouts and curses from the crowd, and it took the marshal several more minutes to bring them under control.

"I think we've heard enough," Lavinia Thurlong cried. "This is no preacher. This man is a charlatan. A fraud. And he has played us for a pack of fools. I say we vote to banish him from Hanging Tree forever. We are good, decent people who deserve better."

Lavinia's friend Gladys and several other women joined in the chorus, whipping the crowd into a frenzy, demanding an immediate vote.

Suddenly their shouting was interrupted by the widow Purdy, leaning heavily on the arm of Doc Prentice and her daughter, Martha.

"Ma refused to stay in her bed," Martha said to the crowd. "She told Doc and me that she wasn't going to meet her Maker until she had a chance to set things right with Reverend Weston here."

"She'd be a fool to pin her hopes on an imposter like him," Lavinia said, to a roar of approval from the crowd.

"You hush now," Doc said in his most professional tone. He turned to Nevada. "I told Mrs. Purdy it'd be a miracle if she lived long enough to say whatever she has on her mind. But it looks like she's about to have her miracle."

"But I . . ." Nevada began.

"No time to jawbone," Doc said with a trace of impatience. "Time's wasting." He lowered the old woman to a rocking chair, while her daughter stuffed several pillows around her to cushion her frail bones.

"Come here, young man," the old woman commanded.

When Mrs. Purdy held out her hand, Nevada approached hesitantly. The woman's eyes followed his every movement.

"I knew I'd get this chance," she whispered.

"Then you knew more than I," he said softly. "I'm sorry you had to suffer like this, Mrs. Purdy. But it was in vain. You see, I'm not—"

"You're not going to say a word," she interrupted. "I just want you to listen."

"But you don't understand." He tried again. "I don't deserve..."

She held up a hand to stop him. "What I have to say is the most important thing you or this town will ever hear. Now, you listen." Pinning Nevada with a look, she said, "You asked me once if this town had ever hanged anyone who didn't deserve it. And I told you no. But I lied. And I can't meet my Maker with a lie on my conscience."

The crowd gave a collective gasp and suddenly leaned forward, hanging on her every word.

"You asked me about a rancher named Jessie Simpson, and I said I couldn't recall the name. The fact is, all the old-timers around here remember Jessie," she said softly. "His was the only hanging I know of that was a mistake."

Jade watched the change in Nevada's face. The look of puzzlement turned into a hard, tight line, his jaw clenched, his gaze fixed on the old woman.

Mrs. Purdy stared around at this collection of friends and neighbors. "Jessie Simpson had a poor ranch not far from the Jewel property. Old Sheriff Handley arrested Jessie for killing a neighboring rancher and rustling his cattle. Jessie insisted he had had no part in it. He even invited the sheriff to search his property."

"Did the sheriff find any cattle?" Doc asked, clearly caught up in her narrative. This was a part of Hanging Tree's history he'd never heard before.

"Not a one. But that didn't change anyone's mind. You see, it hadn't been the first murder, or the first theft of cattle, and folks around here were feeling mean and ornery. Sort of the way they've been these past couple of months, since the Garland Gang returned. People tend to get that way when things start going wrong. Anyhow, folks wanted revenge. Some argued that Jessie could have hidden the stolen herd somewhere out in the foothills. The proof, they said, was that they'd found a cow slaughtered not a mile from his place. Within a week, despite Jessie's protests of innocence, the town had their hanging. And a fine, festive picnic it was. Ranchers came from miles around. I guess the only ones who weren't enjoying themselves were Jessie's family. His wife and young ones were forced to watch the gruesome sight."

That caused some in the crowd to shudder.

"Sounds like just another hanging to me," Lavinia shouted.

The widow ignored Lavinia and the crowd, keeping her gaze fixed on Nevada's face. "Not two weeks after the hanging, another rancher was killed in the same bloody manner, and his cattle stolen. A month later there was another. By then, folks were forced to admit the truth. The same man that killed those others surely had killed Jessie's neighbor. And that meant this fine, upright town, which so many of us had been so proud of, had hanged the wrong man. An innocent man.''

"You can't be sure of that," Lavinia interrupted.

The marshal shot her a quelling look, then asked, "Did anyone from the town go to the Simpson family and try to make amends?''

"They all knew it was too late for that. Jessie was dead and buried, and no amount of being sorry would bring him back. Besides, by then his young widow had run off. Rumor was that she took her babies with her and left her boy to fend for himself.''

At her words, Jade felt her heart stop. She had heard all this before. From Nevada's own lips. But he hadn't told her the most important fact of all—that his father had died by hanging. And that he'd been forced to witness it.

"Did they ever catch the real killer?" Doc Prentice asked.

The widow shook her head. "Everyone suspected Tucker Brand, a rancher who lived alone in a little shack up in the hills.''

"What about the sheriff?" Doc asked. "Did he confront this...Tucker Brand with what he suspected?''

The old woman shook her head sadly. "The sheriff was getting on in years. Winter was coming. Nothing could persuade him to go up into those hills and face Tucker's guns. And the townspeople were too afraid of Tucker to go after him without the law to back them up.''

"You mean no one stopped the killer?" Lavinia stared around at the crowd of friends and neighbors, who had lapsed into an ominous silence.

Jade's eyes were fixed on Nevada's face. A face filled with pain.

Mrs. Purdy lowered her voice. "One night, maybe six months later when the snow melted, Tucker was found dead, his shack burned, his cattle run off.''

"Who do you suppose had the nerve to find and kill him?" Doc asked.

The old woman's voice trembled. "The rumor was that it was Jessie's little boy. No one knew for sure. The boy was never seen in these parts again."

Though Jade had listened in silence, she now asked in a trembling voice, "Mrs. Purdy, what was the boy's name?"

"Danny," the old woman said. "Danny Simpson."

Though she had already guessed the truth, Jade let out a cry and covered her mouth with her hand.

Nevada turned. Their eyes met. He saw hers fill with tears.

The old woman's voice broke into their thoughts. "The townspeople were filled with such shame they vowed to never speak of the incident again. No one went near the Simpson ranch. It was allowed to fall into disrepair. Yancy Winslow was so enraged by what the town had done, he chopped down the hanging tree, hoping that would stop the hangings once and for all. But of course it didn't. Younger folks, not knowing about the past, carried on the tradition. And with every hanging I found myself asking if it could have been prevented, if only we had admitted our past mistake. But no one wanted to be the one to break the code of silence."

"That's all well and good," Lavinia said, pushing her way to the front of the crowd, hoping to regain their confidence. "But it happened a lifetime ago. I don't see what this has to do with any of us."

"Don't you?" The old woman's voice wavered for a moment, then grew stronger. "We call ourselves good, God-fearing people. And then we stand in judgment of others. But some day it will be our turn to be judged. I know when it's my day, I'll hope not for justice but for mercy."

She held out her hand to the young preacher who stood beside her chair. "I hope you will show mercy to those who wronged you and your family."

When he didn't respond she said in a trembling voice, "Did you think I didn't recognize you?"

A murmur went up from the crowd as a few of them began to make sense of all this.

Nevada shook his head. "I was only eight years old."

"And forced to grow up far too soon." She squeezed his hand. "I'm truly sorry, Danny."

"Danny?" Lavinia's brows shot up. "This is the son of the rancher who was hanged?"

"The same," Mrs. Purdy said, keeping her gaze firmly fixed on him. "Lord knows what he's had to suffer because of our mistake. I hope you'll forgive me, Danny. And the rest of this town."

Lavinia's anger exploded. "You want his forgiveness? What about us? What about the fact that he was part of a vicious gang? Why, even his name was a lie. His whole life has been a lie. Do you know where he's been these past weeks, and who he's been with?"

"No," the widow said softly. "And I don't care. Though I fervently hope he was with someone who would ease some of his pain. The only thing that matters is that the Lord brought him back in time to hear my confession. And if Danny forgives me, I will die a happy woman."

"Mrs. Purdy, there's nothing to forgive," Nevada said.

"But there is. We sinned against you and your family," the old woman persisted.

"And I retaliated by sinning against everybody." Nevada's voice carried over the crowd. "The Bible says that unless we admit our mistakes and repent them, we're condemned to repeat them. Since Mrs. Purdy has already had her say, I'll take this moment to have mine. When I was eight years old I was filled with rage. Not only at this town, but at Tucker Brand, who killed and rustled, and who was the

cause of my father's death. But Tucker's crimes
didn't end there. After we were left without my
father's protection, Tucker returned to our ranch and
forced himself on my mother. That's why she ran off
with the first man to offer her a chance to escape.
And why she left me behind. I'd been a witness to her
shame. Each time she looked at me, she felt the pain
and humiliation all over again."

The crowd had gone eerily silent. Many hung their
heads, avoiding eye contact with their neighbors, or
with the man who'd been unjustly forced to deal with
such hardships in his life.

Jade felt her heart break. For the little boy, who'd
had no one to turn to when his world collapsed. And
for the man, who was still standing alone against an
entire town.

"I think," Doc Prentice said aloud, "that we
should ask the reverend's forgiveness for the wrongs
this town committed. I, for one, would ask him to
stay on as minister of Hanging Tree."

"What he's told us doesn't change a thing," Lavinia shouted above the rumble of voices. "He's still
a man who preaches peace while practicing violence."

"She's right," Nevada said. "I had thought I
could turn my back on my old life. But when Ned's
gang of outlaws, my former gang, shot the stage
driver and kidnapped Jade, I wasn't strong enough
to rely on faith alone. I resorted to the only thing
they respected. Guns."

"If that's a fault," Marshal Regan said, "then I should be condemned, too. I don't know much about preaching. But I know a lot about outlaws and violence. And I know what that gang would have done if they'd been allowed to continue their reign of terror. If the reverend hadn't stopped them, who knows which one of us would have been their next victim? I think the town of Hanging Tree is indebted to the reverend for what he did. And I hope you good folks will ask him to stay."

"I want you to stay, Reverend," Mrs. Purdy said. "Not just for my sake, though it would comfort me to have you here until I leave this world. But for the sake of my daughter and all the others I leave behind in Hanging Tree, I hope this town welcomes you back. It's clear that you've become a man of love and compassion. A man worthy to be called reverend."

"I agree with the widow Purdy," Doc Prentice said above the roar of voices. "He's been fair and honest with us. And that's more than many of us can say about our own behavior."

Despite Lavinia's objections, Rufus Durfee called for a vote. One by one the hands went up. Jade watched as Millie Potter and her three daughters lifted their hands. Rufus Durfee raised his hand, followed by his sons, Amos and Damon. The marshal joined them, and Doc Prentice, along with Farley Duke and Samuel Fisher and his wife and four boys. Soon the entire town was voting in the affirmative.

Lavinia and Gladys exchanged looks, then reluctantly lifted their hands to make it unanimous.

With a smile Rufus announced, "Looks like you've got a few friends, Reverend. The whole town of Hanging Tree would like the Reverend Wade Weston...I mean, the Reverend Danny Simpson, to stay on and minister to their needs."

The widow Purdy squeezed Nevada's hand, then hugged her daughter. Doc Prentice and Marshal Regan clapped Nevada on the shoulder.

Jade, her smile radiant, whispered, "Now do you believe in miracles?"

Before he could reply, the crowd surged forward to offer their congratulations.

Nevada surprised them all by raising his hands and calling for silence. When the crowd finally settled down, he said, "I want you to know how much I appreciate your vote of confidence. It's something I'll carry forever in my heart."

"You make it sound like you're leaving," Mrs. Purdy said.

He nodded. "I'm afraid so." Out of the corner of his eye he saw the wounded look on Jade's face. It took all his willpower to keep from reaching out to her. He knew his words would cause her pain. But there was no other way to do this. It would be quick, clean, final. Wasn't that what he'd tried to do in San Francisco, when he'd taken his unexpected leave?

"I'm sorry you went through all this for nothing," he said. "But you never asked me if I wanted to stay."

"It's because of the past, isn't it?" Mrs. Purdy asked. "You can't really forgive us."

He shook his head. "Believe me when I say that I've finally managed to put the past behind me. But it's time I moved on."

The murmur of voices began to grow, until he lifted his hands for silence. "Before I go, I would ask one favor."

The crowd fell silent.

He glanced at Jade, then away. The sorrow in her eyes was too painful to see. In a loud, clear voice he said, "I hope you will remember the danger of becoming a mob. And that you will show compassion to Miss Jade Jewel, even if you disagree with her plans for her new building."

"You see," Lavinia shouted, jumping to her feet. "Even now he's trying to use his influence to protect that...woman."

He nodded. "Just as I'd use my influence to help you, Lavinia, if you ever needed it." He turned to the marshal. "I'm trusting you to protect Miss Jewel, no matter how you may disagree with her."

Marshal Regan nodded. "You can count on it, Reverend."

Nevada shook his hand. Then, with a quick wave, he started through the crowd. With shouts of good luck and Godspeed, many reached out to shake his hand, or to clap him on the shoulder.

As he walked out the door, Jade hurried after him. Outside, he was pulling himself into the saddle.

"Were you going to leave without a word to me?" she cried.

"I think it's best." He hated himself. But there was no turning back now. Quick and clean. It was the only way he'd get through it. "Goodbye, Jade. I hope..." No. He wouldn't ask her to think of him. He had no right to ask anything of her. "You know that I wish you...only the best."

He nudged his horse into a trot. And refused to look back.

Jade stood on the wooden walkway and watched through a blur of tears as he rode out of town. And out of her life.

Chapter Twenty-Two

A storm was threatening. Already thunder rumbled in the distance.

Nevada stared around the little cabin, strewn with broken furniture and bits of pottery. He'd needed to come here one last time. To say goodbye to his past and contemplate his future.

He piled logs on the grate and started a fire with kindling, then stood, wiping his hands on his pants.

He still couldn't believe he'd just turned his back on everything he'd ever wanted. It was all there in the little town of Hanging Tree. With the widow Purdy's admission of wrongdoing, his family name had been vindicated. The vote of confidence by the townspeople had restored his integrity, his self-respect. And most important of all, the woman he loved was in that town.

The woman he loved.

He had to close his eyes against the pain. Their situation was impossible. The minister and the madam. Still, as impossible as it was, he was tormented by thoughts of what his life would be like without her.

All his life he'd mourned the loss of his family. And though he'd tried to deny it, he'd begun to weave dreams about Jade. Impossible dreams, of course. But that didn't stop them from spinning around in his head. Dreams of her as his wife, making a home for him, even having his children.

What nonsense. Next he'd be picturing her giving up the opulent life-style she'd been born to and ministering alongside him to the people of Hanging Tree. For that was how he wanted to spend the rest of his life. As a simple preacher. It was the work he was meant to do. No one better understood pain and anger and the healing power of forgiveness than a man who had paid so dearly for his mistakes. But Jade's life was another story. She'd been trained to offer healing of a different sort.

He picked up another log and tossed it onto the fire with a vengeance, causing sparks to leap and dance. The thunder was closer now, and he thought he heard the spattering of raindrops.

He should have kept right on riding until he was clear out of Texas. It had been a mistake to stop here. There were too many memories. Too much pain. And he was helpless to do anything about it.

His head came up. What he'd first thought to be the sound of rain was now clearly distinguishable. A team and carriage. Approaching at a run.

He hurried to the small window and watched as a slender figure raced through the downpour.

A moment later the door was thrown open and Jade hurried inside, closing the door against a rush of wind.

She leaned against the door, taking several deep breaths. Her silk gown was rain spattered, her hair wind tossed.

"I should have known this was your cabin." Her voice trembled. "From the look in your eyes that first time we walked in. And from all the feelings that were still so alive, so unsettled in this place. I could feel them like ghosts. But it wasn't until now that I put it all together."

"You shouldn't have come." He stayed where he was. It would be dangerous to get close to her. He'd never have the strength to walk away again. "We've already said our goodbyes."

"No," she said quickly. "You said yours. But you gave me no chance to say mine." She took in another deep breath and struggled to calm her jumping nerves. She'd been so afraid he wouldn't be here. So afraid that her last chance would be lost. And now that she was here with him, she was terrified.

"Something happened last night," she said softly. "After everyone was asleep, I came into town. It was my intention to come to you, to make you see that, however impossible our situation, we could find a way to be together. But something caused me to stop first to see the progress of my building. And while I was there I had a visitor. A visitor who changed my life."

"I don't under—"

"Birdie Bidwell came to see me about a job."

His puzzled look turned to one of outrage. "But she's only—"

"I know. A child. But a desperate one, willing to do anything necessary to help her family. And that made me realize that I couldn't turn my back on her. Or on anyone else who needed my help."

"Are you telling me you're going to hire her?" His voice was low with fury.

Jade gave him a strange, mysterious smile. "You say you're leaving Hanging Tree. But it's obvious that you still care very much about its people."

"Answer me," he demanded. "Are you going to hire Birdie?"

"That depends on you."

When he arched a brow in surprise, she said softly, "Lavinia Thurlong once told me that what the town of Hanging Tree really needed was a house of worship, not a house of pleasure. I hate to say it, but Lavinia is right. And since I've just built a very big structure, it just might serve the purpose. That is, if you wouldn't mind living above a church."

He studied her face for some sign that she was teasing. "You're offering me the Golden Dragon...as a church?"

"I am. Of course," she went on, "there are some stipulations."

"Such as?"

"I'm thinking of calling it the Golden Rule."

"The Golden . . . Rule?"

"I hate waste," she said, her expression serious. "And the workmen have already painted in the word *Golden* in very expensive gold leaf."

"I see." Nevada was struggling not to laugh. "It wouldn't occur to you to just cover up the word *Golden* with a few swipes of paint?"

She shrugged. "I'll need time to think about it. But it's possible, if you prefer another name. Now, there is another stipulation. The building is very big. You might want to use some of the rooms for other things, like town socials and meeting halls, instead of using Durfee's Mercantile."

"I think that's wise. However, all of this sounds like a pretty big undertaking." He tried to look as serious as Jade. "I might need an assistant. Do you know of anyone who'd be up to the task of seeing to all those socials and meetings and such?"

She took a step closer and saw the way his gaze was drawn to the sway of her hips. That gave her the courage to draw even closer. "I know of someone who had an excellent tutor," she said with a straight face. "A woman who was groomed for a life of service."

"Is church work the sort of service her tutor had in mind?"

She shrugged. "Service is service. Of course, she would need some help."

"Help?"

Jade nodded. "That's where Birdie Bidwell comes in. She's very good at cooking and cleaning. And there may be other youngsters in the town in need of steady employment. You might want to think about hiring them, as well."

"You have a very devious mind, Miss Jewel. But very efficient. As usual, it looks like you've thought of everything," Nevada muttered. "Of course, there is just one problem. The assistant you have in mind is quite acceptable to me. But I don't think the town would approve of the two of us sharing that church building without benefit of marriage. You see, a preacher can't have an . . . arrangement. So it would have to be marriage or nothing."

"Oh," she said with a look of complete innocence. "Didn't I mention that?"

"I guess you forgot."

She took another step until she was directly in front of him. Lifting a hand, she smoothed the collar of his shirt. "You'd have to marry your assistant. It's the only thing a woman like that would consider."

"A woman like that?"

"Mmm-hmm. A woman like that." She couldn't help it. The words brought a smile to her lips.

His mouth opened, but no words came out. He'd just been handed the most precious gift of all.

"And I'd like children," she added, growing bolder. "At least four or five. You see, until I discovered three sisters here in Hanging Tree, I was an only child, and I always thought it a lonely life.''

"I see.'' He dared to touch a finger to her lips. At once he felt the flare of heat. He traced the outline of her lips, before his fingertips rested on her cheek.

She felt the jolt clear to her toes.

"I know this sounds like a lot, but it has to be all proper and legal.'' She knew she was jabbering, but she couldn't seem to stop. Not when he was touching her like this.

"Proper and legal?'' He pretended to contemplate, all the while watching her eyes. Sweet heaven, how was it possible to love one little woman so much?

"Well?'' She gave him what she hoped was a challenging look. "What do you have to say?''

Instead of words, he dragged her against him and covered her mouth with his. The kiss was hot and hungry, and filled with such need it sent her heart spiraling out of control.

She pushed a little away. "I guess that means yes.''

"Yes,'' he muttered. "Yes. Definitely yes.''

"Then we'd better get back to town and tell everybody that they have their preacher back. When I left, they were all bemoaning their loss.''

He dragged her close and kissed her again, this time long and slow and deep. "Tomorrow is soon enough,'' he breathed inside her mouth. "It isn't a fit night to be out in that storm.''

"You mean ... ?''

"Mmm-hmm." His mouth nibbled hers until she sighed with pleasure. "Looks like we're stuck here until morning."

Jade blinked to hide the tears that sprang to her eyes. At this moment her heart was so full of joy she thought it would surely burst.

"Danny Simpson, you belong here, in the town that once shunned you," she whispered. "You need these people as much as they need you."

"And it's only right that Onyx Jewel's daughter should find happiness in the land that nurtured her honorable father."

She wrapped her arms around his neck and gave herself up to his kisses.

Together they would heal all the old wounds. And mend some broken hearts. Starting with their own. Right this very minute.

Epilogue

"Jade," Pearl commanded. "Hold still while I finish your hair." She twined ivy and delicate wildflowers through Jade's ebony tresses.

"Stop wiggling, *chérie*," Ruby said sharply, "so I don't stick you with this needle." She put the finishing touches on Jade's gown, then stepped back to study the bride with a critical eye.

"Wait till you see the wedding supper the ladies of the town have prepared." Diamond, just stepping into the room with a bouquet of wildflowers, turned around and stopped in midstride. "Oh, my," was all she could manage. Then, recovering, she said, "I almost forgot. There's a man outside your room. Insists he has to see you right away. But I told him it wasn't proper for the groom to see the bride before the wedding."

"Nevada." Jade started toward the door with a laugh of delight.

"I think you'd better get used to calling him Dan," Diamond said dryly. "It wouldn't do for the town preacher to be called by an outlaw's name."

"I suppose you're right," Jade said, coming to a halt. "But it was Nevada I fell in love with on my sixteenth birthday."

"And I hope I'm still the one you love when you're one hundred," he said, striding into the room without waiting for an invitation.

"You know what I told you . . ." Diamond began. But a look from Jade had her shaking her head in defeat. She signaled her sisters, and the three of them left the happy couple alone.

He closed the door and leaned against it, studying the woman who stood facing him. Her gown of white silk, with silver frog fasteners, skimmed her body and fell to the tips of white kid slippers. Her only jewelry was her father's gift to her, the rope of gold on which dangled onyx and jade. Her dark hair, dressed with ivy and wildflowers, had been pulled to one side with his mother's comb and spilled over her breast. He felt as he had that first time, when he'd seen her in the Golden Dragon in San Francisco. She was so lovely she took his breath away.

"Have any guests arrived yet?" she asked shyly.

"Only the entire town. Even Lavinia, and her daughter, Agnes, who brought her latest cowboy. Doesn't anyone bother to stay at home and do their chores?"

She smiled. "You're sounding almost grumpy. Do I detect nerves, Reverend?"

He jammed his hands into his pockets to keep from touching her. "I don't understand it. I've preached a hundred times or more. It's never bothered me before. And today I don't even have to give a sermon. All that's required is a few simple words. But I've been up since dawn, just trying to remember my name."

"I can understand why. You've had so many. Would you prefer Reverend Simpson?" she asked, stepping close enough to skim a hand down his arm. "Or Dan?"

He closed his hand over hers. Sunlight spilling through the window turned his amber eyes to flame. "How about calling me—" he drew her into the circle of his arms and brushed her lips with his "—husband?"

At once all the pent-up passion brought a rush of heat that left them weak.

"It's what I want more than anything."

"And I want you." He kissed her until she was breathless. "Only you, Jade. I want—"

The door was thrown open, and Diamond whispered fiercely, "The guests are starting to fidget. You'd better get downstairs fast." Seeing what she'd interrupted, she said lamely, "Oh. Sorry. But the children are eyeing those cakes and pies. There won't be any left if you don't hurry."

"All right," Nevada said through gritted teeth. "We'll be right down."

When the door closed he pressed his forehead against Jade's. "Now, where was I?" He began nibbling her temple, her cheek, her ear. "Oh, yes. I remember. I want—"

The door was thrown open again, and Ruby whispered, "*Chérie.* You will have the rest of your life for that. Right now you must hurry. The men have just hung the bell on the top of the building and they have worked up a tremendous appetite. They are threatening to eat everything before the service even begins."

"Bell?" Jade and Nevada asked in unison.

"Oh." She clapped a hand over her mouth. "It was to be a surprise. It is your wedding gift from the townspeople. So that you can call them to meetings."

When the door closed, Jade took one look at Nevada's face and burst into laughter.

"What's so funny?" he demanded.

"You," she said, laughing even harder. "If you intend to minister to the needs of the entire town, you'd better get used to surprises. And interruptions."

"But can't a man have a few minutes alone with his bride?"

"Almost bride," she reminded him. "And if we don't get downstairs soon, there won't be time for the wedding."

With a sigh he offered his arm. As she linked her arm to his, she studied his strong, proud profile. He looked just as she remembered from the first time she'd seen him. Handsome. Mysterious. And hers. All hers.

He turned to her, and her heart stopped.

"I love you, Jade. With all my heart and soul. And I promise you that I'll do everything in my power to make you happy."

As they started down the stairs toward the waiting throng, she felt her heart overflowing with happiness. And as they spoke their vows to one another, he removed a ring from his pocket and slipped it on her finger. A ring of twisted gold, with an amber stone that caught and reflected the light of hundreds of candles.

"This was the only thing of value my father had to give me," he murmured. "And I give it to you, Jade, along with my heart."

She stared at the symbol of his love through a shimmer of tears. "You're wrong," she whispered. "Your father left something much more valuable. You, to restore his family name to its rightful place of honor."

When the vows were spoken, they drew together in a tender kiss, while the crowd murmured their approval.

Oh, honorable Father. You knew all along, didn't you? You were right here by my side the whole time. The legacy you left me was not one of loneliness.

Instead, you found a way for me to have it all. Satisfying work. A chance to remain here in Texas with my new sisters. And best of all, the man of my dreams.

Her tutor had been wrong. Man was not her enemy. Nor was he a necessary evil. He was her heart's desire. The love of her life.

With Nevada, the Reverend Dan Simpson, as her husband, she was prepared for everything the future had to offer.

For love, true and enduring love, really was the greatest adventure of all.

* * * * *

IT'S THAT TIME OF YEAR AGAIN!

You are cordially invited to a

HOMETOWN REUNION

September 1996—August 1997

Bad boys, cowboys, babies. Feuding families,
arson, mistaken identity, a mom on the run...
Where can you find romance and adventure?
Tyler, Wisconsin, that's where!

So join us in this not-so-sleepy little town and
experience the love, the laughter and the
tears of those who call it home.

WELCOME TO A
HOMETOWN REUNION

Gabe Atwood has no sooner rescued his wife,
Raine, from a burning building when there's
more talk of fires. Rumor has it that Clint
Stanford suspects Jon Weiss, the new kid at
school, of burning down the Ingallses' factory.
And that Marina, Jon's mother, has kindled a fire
in Clint that may be affecting his judgment. Don't
miss Kristine Rolofson's *A Touch of Texas*,
the seventh in a series you won't want to end....

Available in March 1997
at your favorite retail store.

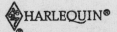

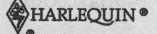

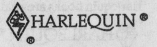